the trouble with rules

For Mia and Zeke

Published by
PEACHTREE PUBLISHERS
1700 Chattahoochee Avenue
Atlanta, Georgia 30318-2112

www.peachtree-online.com

Text © 2008 by Leslie Bulion

First trade paperback edition published in 2011

Cover design by Maureen Withee
Book design by Melanie McMahon Ives

Manufactured in March 2011 in Bloomsburg, PA by R.R. Donnelley & Sons
in the United States of America
10 9 8 7 6 5 4 3 2 (hardcover)
10 9 8 7 6 5 4 3 2 1 (trade paperback)

Library of Congress Cataloging-in-Publication Data

Bulion, Leslie, 1958-
  The trouble with rules / by Leslie Bulion. -- 1st ed.
    p. cm.
  Summary: Now that she is in fourth grade and is not supposed to be friends with boys any-more, Nadie must hide her friendship with Nick, her neighbor and lifelong best friend, but when a new girl arrives who believes that some rules need to be broken, Nadie learns a lot from her.
  ISBN 13: 978-1-56145-440-2 / ISBN 10: 1-56145-440-0 (hardcover)
  ISBN 13: 978-1-56145-576-8 / ISBN 10: 1-56145-576-8 (trade paperback)
  [1. Best friends--Fiction. 2. Friendship--Fiction. 3. Schools--Fiction. 4. Interpersonal relations--Fiction. 5. Family life--Fiction.] I. Title.
  PZ7.B911155Br 2008
  [Fic]--dc22
                                    2007039687

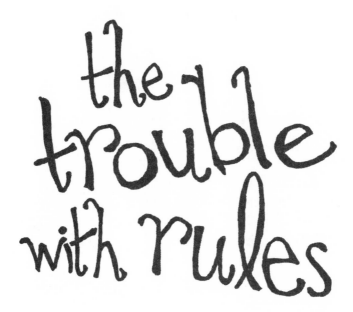

the trouble with rules

Leslie Bulion

PEACHTREE
ATLANTA

Acknowledgments

With ongoing and tremendous gratitude to my writing buddies and my family for their critical input, support, and encouragement. Thanks to Steven C. for his close reading and suggestions. So many thanks to the enthusiastic and remarkably kind staff at Peachtree, and especially to my editor, Vicky Holifield, and copy editor, Amy Brittain. And thank you, Patrick M., for starting me off with those pencils.

Contents

1

PENCILS

The new girl blew into Room Twenty on a whoosh of air as cool as the spaces between snowflakes. She smelled a little like cats.

I noticed the smell right away because of my uncle's cat, Francis. When we're visiting my uncle, Francis glares at my brother and me from the bedroom doorway the whole time. That cat is always hatching an evil plot, which is why I don't trust cats.

Mr. Allen walked over to our four-desk group and pushed an empty desk so the front of it touched the sides of mine and Nick's. On the other side of Nick, Owen picked up two of those pink eraser caps that normal people use on the ends of their pencils and got busy. Busy sticking them in his nose, that is.

"Eeew!" Lacey squealed in my ear. "Don't look, Nadie!" She covered her face.

I looked. It's always a good idea to keep an eye on Owen. He hauled in a gigantic breath and snorted. The erasers shot out: *thoop-thoop*. He crawled under his desk after them, then put them back on his pencils. It's also a good idea never to touch anything that belongs to Owen if you can help it.

"Fellow learners," Mr. Allen said in his attention-please voice. "This is Summer Crawford." He put his long arm around the new girl's shoulders and steered her to the empty desk. "She'll be joining our class for the rest of the year. I'm sure you will all help her feel welcome." Mr. Allen raised one sharp, black eyebrow at Owen, then turned back to the new girl.

Owen ducked behind his desk lid. When he picked his head up for a second, I saw that the erasers were back in his nose, this time with the pencils attached. He ducked back down. There was another snort, and then *thoop-ding, thoop-ding*, the pencils hit the inside of his desk. It's a good thing Owen's desk is diagonally across from mine so I never have to look inside there.

"Owen," Mr. Allen said. "I think—"

We never got to hear what Mr. Allen thought because right then our principal, Mrs. Winger, opened the classroom door. She motioned to Mr. Allen.

"I need to step outside with Mrs. Winger for a moment," Mr. Allen said. "Let's help Summer feel welcome with our excellent Room Twenty behavior." Mr. Allen went into the hall and closed the door behind him.

The new girl bent at the waist and shimmied out of an enormously wooly sweater. Her shirt hiked up under her arms, and we all got a good look at her wide, pale back. Right in the middle was a brown beauty mark that looked like Louisiana, and bunching up from the waistband of her jeans, a shiny roll of purple underwear.

"Eww—your shirt!" squealed Lacey.

The new girl tugged her shirt back down, then flumped into her seat. The tips of her hair fluttered against her chin like dry grass. She smiled all around as if one of the most embarrassing things in the world hadn't just happened to her.

"Hi," she said, sticking her hand right out at Nick. "I'm Summer."

Nick's face filled in pink between his freckles. The room got so quiet I figured everyone had quit breathing.

Maybe they went by different rules in Summer's last school. We sure did last year in third grade, when we were in the lower primary school, next door. But here in Upper Springville Elementary, boys and girls in the fourth grade barely talked to each other. And they definitely didn't shake hands.

Every eye in the room was trained right on Nick. He gulped. He slouched down small in his seat. He coughed and scratched his knee. Then he reached out and gave Summer's hand a quick pump. "Nick," he mumbled.

"Oooh!" Lacey whispered loud enough to be heard in China. "Nick likes the new girl!" She jabbed me with her bony elbow. I edged away from her.

"Love at first sight!" Max yelled from the back of the room.

At the next group of desks, Alima and Jess giggled.

Owen stood up, pointed his finger at the back of his throat, and made gagging noises. Other kids laughed. As if she didn't notice any of it, Summer lifted her desk lid and started putting away her pencils and folders. Nick just sat there looking miserable. Nick says he is *not* too nice for his own good, but he is, and shaking hands with the new girl like that was a perfect example. He knew that Owen would make fun of him. Now Owen was going to keep making fun of him until the whole class joined in.

In school we had to act like we hardly knew each other, but

3

Nick Fanelli was my best friend. I had to do something to help him.

Through the glass in the door I could see Mrs. Winger's hands waving as she talked. Mr. Allen was nodding. Owen gagged again, louder, to make sure he had every kid's full attention. I needed to distract them. Maybe I could fold up a supersonic paper jet. A good one could loop all the way up to the ceiling, then shoot across the room. But a paper airplane could get me into trouble, and besides, it would take too much time to make one. I needed a better plan. I decided to pretend I was choking. As far as I knew, choking wasn't against any rule, and I could do that right at my desk. Out in the hall, Mr. Allen was doing the talking and Mrs. Winger was listening. It was now or never. I coughed and wheezed, making the sounds as scary as possible, then put my hands around my throat. With a loud gasp I tipped sideways off my chair.

Slam! Summer's desk lid dropped shut. The room went silent. From where I was lying on the floor I craned my head around to look. Summer had a pencil poking out of each ear, a pencil dangling from each nostril, and four more pencils jutting from her mouth like long yellow fangs. She had flipped her eyelids inside out for good measure.

Lacey screamed. Max leaped out of his chair. "Gross!" he shouted. "Ugh!" Alima and Jess wailed. The rest of the kids hooted and hollered.

The door swung open and hit the wall—*bang!* I pulled myself up into my chair. Everyone stopped still. You could hear the clock tick. I stared down at my desktop, letting the long brown curtain of my hair fall forward to hide my face. Mr. Allen's purple high-top sneakers squeaked across the room and came to a halt right beside my desk.

4

My heart beat a *rat-a-tat-tat*, louder than the snare drum in band. I wondered if I could climb into my desk and shut the lid behind me. Next I wondered if Summer and I would be visiting Mrs. Winger's office singly or together. Did they send two kids at a time? I didn't know. I'd never been in visit-the-principal's-office trouble before.

"Is everything all right in here?" Mr. Allen asked. I examined the worn-in scratches on my desktop and swallowed hard. I didn't look at Nick, and I definitely didn't look at Summer Crawford, pencil queen.

"Just fine," Summer said.

I screwed my eyes shut. Well, that solved one half of the mystery. With her yellow fangs and the rest of it, Summer was definitely going to see Mrs. Winger. Under our desks, Nick poked my knee with his foot. I ignored him. He planted his foot on my knee and shoved. I opened one eye. Eight pencils with their big fat erasers on the tops lay in a neat line on Summer's desk. Her eyelids were right side out.

"I feel at home here already," Summer told Mr. Allen. She smiled so big she showed all of her teeth.

"Wonderful!" Mr. Allen bobbed his head up and down. "Better than marvelous!" He rubbed his hands together. "Now let's get on with our morning work. Math first."

Every kid in our class let out one long breath. Everybody, that is, except Owen. He just stared at Summer. He stared so hard I thought he might stare a hole right through to the other side of her.

"Need a pencil?" Summer asked him.

Owen opened his mouth, closed it, then opened it again like he wanted to yell, except his voice wouldn't cooperate. Nick bit his lip and buried his nose in his math book so that all you could see of him was his short red hair. I knew Nick wasn't worrying about that handshake anymore, and he wasn't worrying about long division.

He was worrying about what was going to happen now that Summer Crawford was here.

2
THE BOYS' SIDE

Gather your edible matter, fellow scientists," Mr. Allen announced just before noon. "I'm due at a meeting in Mrs. Winger's office in three and a half minutes."

I shot my hand into the air. "But what about our *Springville Spark* editorial meeting?" I asked.

Mr. Allen got up from his desk. "I'm sorry. We'll have to cancel it today. We're going to have some free time this afternoon, and we'll finish this week's issue then. We'll celebrate our study of space with this issue before we zoom back to Earth for our new science unit on insects. Now, let's form our exemplary Room Twenty lunchroom line."

Nick put his meal ticket in his pocket and trudged over to the line forming by the door. I dug around in my desk for my brown paper bag. It didn't matter about the *Spark*, not really. We could finish the class magazine at free time. The problem was that instead of eating lunch together in the classroom, Nick and I would have to eat at separate tables in the zoofeteria.

I wished lunch could be the way it had been in third grade. I'd always sat with Nick. But in upper school's lunch, the cafeteria was divided down the middle by an invisible wall—boys on the window side, and girls on the side near the hall. Now

I'd have to sit with Lacey, Alima, and Jess, and Nick would be stuck all the way across the room at a table with Owen, Max, and some other boys.

I got in line behind Summer and followed her out into the hall. She was pulling her big sweater over her head. The faint smell of cat drifted my way, and of course I thought of that horrid Francis again. If you ask my almost-three-year-old brother Zack what a kitty says, he growls and hisses because that's what Francis does.

"You don't need that," I said to Summer, whose head was still somewhere inside her sweater. Winter had just turned the corner to April, but a sky the color of dirty dishwater hung over the playground. "It's still sleeting. We're not going out."

"*I* am." Her head pushed through the neck hole and she shoved her arms into her sleeves.

"You're not allowed to go out by yourself," I told her. "School rules."

"Where's the cafeteria?" She brushed her hair behind her ears. The front parts escaped again right away.

I pointed. "Around that corner."

Summer looked both ways like she was getting ready to cross a street. "See you there," she said, slipping out the play-ground door.

I watched her run across the pavement and duck under the slide. What could she possibly be up to?

"Nadie, please stay with the class."

I jumped about three feet in the air, and I wasn't even the one who'd ignored the rules. The rest of the kids had already disappeared around the corner. Mr. Allen stood waiting for me.

I got on the end of the lunch line without looking at Mr.

Allen, but I could feel him watching me. The sour smell of rubbery franks and beans filled my nose and clogged the back of my throat. *Don't ask about her,* I prayed. *Don't ask, don't ask.*

"Nadie, wasn't Summer back here with you?"

"Ye-es." It came out like a squeak. The lunch line stopped moving. I looked straight ahead as if there was something enormously interesting on the wall outside the lunchroom doorway. All I had to do was get through the door before Mr. Allen asked me anything else. What was holding up the line? Summer might as well have taken a shortcut to Mrs. Winger's office, because that's where she was headed this time for sure. I squeezed past Alima and Jess, trying to get to Lacey.

"Hey!" they complained.

"Nadie?" Mr. Allen's long arm stretched over them and clamped onto my shoulder.

I stopped. "Mr. Allen, I—"

"Did you think you lost her?" He turned me sideways by my shoulder. "She just got ahead of you—look!"

Summer was walking over to the other side of the room, past the lunch monitor, Mrs. Wolfowitz. Mrs. Wolfowitz was shorter than most of us and as wide as a doorway. She always sat on a chair in the middle of the room with her eyes shut for the entire lunch period. We'd learned that she didn't much care what we did as long as we stayed in our seats to do it. The older kids say that a long time ago a fifth grade boy got up before the bell, just to throw something away. "That's it," Mrs. Wolfowitz had said. "Let's go." She took him away. No one saw where he went. The next day the lunch lady was back in her seat in the middle of the lunchroom. But they way they tell it, no one ever saw that fifth grader again.

Mr. Allen still had me by the shoulder. He gave me a little shove toward Summer. "She's certainly learning her way around quickly, isn't she?" he remarked.

I wasn't so sure. Summer had gone outside, run around the building, and sneaked back in through a different lunchroom door. Now she was heading toward an empty table on the other side of Mrs. Wolfowitz—a table on the *boys' side*.

* * *

As I neared her, I could see that droplets clung to Summer's sweater. Her cheeks and nose were the color of supermarket strawberries.

"Got my lunch." She held up a plastic grocery bag. Then she slung one leg over the bench to sit down.

"Summer, wait!" I yelled. But my words drowned in the voices of almost two hundred other Upper Elementary lunchers.

"What?" She plunked herself down on the bench. Then she yanked on my arm and I landed next to her.

"You just sat us on the boys' side," I wailed.

"Boys' side?"

"Yeah. We were supposed to sit over there." I pointed toward the safe area on the other side of Mrs. Wolfowitz.

"You mean girls can't sit here?" Summer peered into her plastic bag. "Who made that stupid rule?"

"I don't know—everybody," I said. "It's just how you have to do it." I glanced from side to side. The way the boys were looking at us, we might as well have been aliens with three purple heads.

"I don't get it." Summer shrugged. "But okay, let's move over to the other side." She closed her bag and started to get up.

"No!" I pulled her back down. "We can't!"

Summer stared at me like I'd gone completely nuts. "Just tell me this," she said. "If we're not supposed to sit *here*, then why can't we go over there?"

"Because once you sit down, you're not supposed to get out of your seat." I pointed at the lunch lady asleep in her chair and lowered my voice. "That's Mrs. Wolfowitz's rule. If you get up, she makes you disappear."

Summer Crawford twisted around and studied the woman in the chair. Then she turned back to me and raised one eyebrow. She took a napkin out of her bag and calmly spread it on her lap.

I could tell she didn't believe me about Mrs. Wolfowitz.

* * *

So far no boys had sat down at our table, and I was beginning to think that I might survive the lunch period after all. I took out the yogurt, the carrot sticks, and the almond butter sandwich with raisins that my dad had packed for me. He's a healthy-food fanatic. He says the three-to-eleven shift my mom works at Brennan Engineering is called the graveyard shift because all the junk they eat will kill you. Lacey thinks my dad and my lunches are not "normal." The last time I had to eat in the lunchroom, she tried to get me to eat those blue and yellow gummy giraffes that stick your teeth together.

"It's fruit," she'd said, pointing to the flashy advertising on the package. "See?"

Looking at Summer's plastic bag, I wondered if she ate those blue and yellow giraffes, too, or what.

"Why'd you have to go outside to get your lunch?" I asked her. I opened my yogurt and gave it a stir.

"Refrigeration," she said. "I used that petrified snowbank by the corner of the playground." She took a family-sized jar of mayonnaise out of her bag. Next came a turkey drumstick big enough to bat a Wiffle ball. It smelled like the day after Thanksgiving. She put the turkey leg on top of the empty bag and opened the jar. Then she ripped off a hunk of meat and used it to scoop out a blob of mayonnaise.

"Mmmm," Summer said, chewing with her eyes closed. Her knuckles were shiny with grease.

Watching her made me want to take a break from eating. I put my yogurt spoon down on my napkin.

Just as Summer tore off another chunk of turkey, Nick walked by. He was so keen on looking straight ahead that he slipped on an empty juice box and almost dropped his tray. Having to pretend we weren't friends this year had been a lot of work for Nick and me. But today it was turning out to be downright dangerous. And I knew Nick was wondering what in the world I was doing sitting on the boys' side. I was wondering the same thing myself.

A loud voice at the other end of our table interrupted my thoughts. "Aw—no other seats." Owen slammed his tray down. "Guess we have to sit here with the cave girls." Max and two of their friends from Mrs. Novotny's class sat with him. They looked over at us and snickered.

"Baked beans," said Owen. "Great ammo!" He blew the wrapper off of his straw and loaded a bean into his shooter. A bean zinged right past his head from the direction of the next table. Owen aimed his straw for a return shot while the others loaded.

Figuring they'd forget about us now, I turned away and took a bite of my sandwich.

"It must take a long time to make all that." Summer waved a piece of her slimed turkey at my lunch. "I'm not what you'd call an early riser, so I go for the grab grub."

"I don't get up early enough to make my lunch either," I said. I felt a little embarrassed. "My dad makes it."

"I don't have a dad."

I stopped chewing.

"Don't worry," Summer said. She gave a little laugh. "It's not like I had one that died or anything. He left before I was even born."

A baked bean flew right by us and smacked into the side of Owen's head. It came from the table on the other side of us, but he must have thought I shot it. "Let's get 'em!" he yelled.

"It wasn't me," I insisted, pointing. "It came from those boys over there." Owen turned his attention to the table next to us, and I looked back at Summer.

I thought about what she'd said about her not having a dad. I held up my carrot sticks. "Want some?" I asked her.

She gave me this funny smile, kind of shy and wide open at the same time. "Thanks," she said, which mostly just looked like her mouth moving because Owen and the others were now in some sort of shouting match.

"Put beans in it!" Max yelled.

13

"I'm putting Jell-O in it, too!" Owen bellowed. "And I'm shaking it up!"

Summer took a couple of carrots and ate them, smiling and chewing at the same time. "Here." She pulled a hunk of turkey off the leg and tipped her mayonnaise jar toward me. "Try some of mine."

I could see greasy globs of mayonnaise shivering on the inside of the glass.

"NOW!" Owen shouted.

He leaned past me and sloshed the contents of his milk carton into Summer's open mayonnaise jar.

"HAH-HAH!" he yelled. The other boys pounded his back and cheered.

Summer screwed the lid on the jar and shook it. Mushed beans and dots of mayonnaise swirled in a foamy pink broth. "Thanks," she told Owen. "I am pretty thirsty." She raised the jar like she was making a toast, then tipped it back and took a swallow. She smiled at the astonished boys through a chalky pink mustache.

"Yah! Gross!" Max slapped the table and high-fived one of the other boys. The rest of them looked like they might be sick.

Owen jumped up. His face was all red. "You—you can't do that!" he yelled.

And just like that the lunch lady was at our table. The rest of the cafeteria suddenly went quiet, as if someone had hit the mute button.

"That's it," said Mrs. Wolfowitz. "Let's go."

3

COLLISION COURSE

M arch!" Mrs. Wolfowitz pointed toward the wall. Owen glared at Summer. She grinned at him. Summer Crawford might think she was funny, but I knew that the look on Owen's face meant trouble.

"Now!" Mrs. Wolfowitz ordered.

Owen stomped off toward the side of the room. Everybody else in the lunchroom sat at their tables and watched him go. There was no talking, no laughing, no slurping, no chewing. The only other sound in the room was the *gurgle-gurgle-gurgle* of the water fountain.

"WHAT ARE THE REST OF YOU WAITING FOR? GET MOVING!"

Max and the two boys from Mrs. Novotny's class got up and slunk over to join Owen at the wall. Summer and I hurried after them double-time.

Mrs. Wolfowitz made us stand in a line with our backs against the side wall. "And stay there until I tell you to move," she warned, then returned to her seat in the center of the room.

We stood there so long I thought I might keel over. I watched the kids at the tables like I was watching a movie of a lunchroom. Or a movie of a teacher's idea of a lunchroom. It was weirdly quiet. All the other kids finished eating their lunches in a kind of careful slow motion. No one looked at us, not even when the bell rang and they had to file out right past where we were standing. They avoided contact with us like they thought our trouble might be contagious. Even Nick didn't look at me. He just blinked and blinked as he walked by. His face was about as white as a freckled face could get.

After everyone else had left, Mrs. Wolfowitz pulled a big ring of keys from her pocket. She marched to the wall next to the food counters and stuck one of the keys into a lock. I'd never noticed a door there before. The door creaked open. It was very dark on the other side.

"Go," she said.

One by one we filed into the darkness. Mrs. Wolfowitz stepped in and slammed the door behind her. I gulped. I shut my eyes and opened them again to make sure my lids were up. They were. Was this how that kid had disappeared? What would Nick tell my dad when I didn't come home today? The smell of wet cat filled my nose and I started on a slow burn. I knew whose fault this was. Owen would always be Owen, but none of this would have happened if it hadn't been for Summer Crawford.

There was a deafening crash. Then a light came on. The first thing I saw in the harsh glare was the lunch lady holding the pull cord from a dangling bulb. Just behind her was Owen, sprawled in a collection of janitor's buckets. Mops stuck out from the wringers at crazy angles.

"Get up," Mrs. Wolfowitz said to him. "Then all of you, in line."

We stood shoulder to shoulder facing the lunch lady. She looked us over, sizing us up for something—jail cells...or worse. The dim bulb swung back and forth with a slow *eek-eek-eek*.

"You!" We all jumped. She was pointing to the bigger boy from Mrs. Novotny's class. He let out a whimper.

"No talking!" Mrs. Wolfowitz grabbed a big trash barrel and pushed it toward him. She handed the short, round-faced boy a broom. Max and I got sponges and spray bottles shoved into our hands. Summer got a dustpan and whisk broom. "You clear off the tables and clean up after the broom boy," the lunch lady said.

"Since you like the buckets so much, you get this." She rolled a bucket at Owen, holding it by its mop. The wheels squeaked and soapy water sloshed around inside. "As soon as the others clear a row, it's your job to mop the floor."

Mrs. Wolfowitz opened the door again. I had never been so glad to see the zoofeteria.

"Clean this place until it sparkles," she said, "and then you can go back to class."

I looked around at the tables gobbed with food. I surveyed the floor, ankle deep in greasy napkins and popped milk cartons. Then I kind of wished she *had* just made us disappear. Forget recess, forget class, and forget free time. It would take hours to clean all this up. It seemed entirely possible that we'd find that missing fifth grader buried under a pile of mushed-up hot dog buns. *Now I get it*, I thought. *We'll never leave here. This actually* is *how Mrs. Wolfowitz makes kids disappear.*

"C'mon, Nadie. I bet we can finish way before these guys," Summer said, louder than she needed to. She looked at Owen and pushed her hair behind her ears.

"No talking!" Mrs. Wolfowitz snapped.

Summer started sweeping trash from the tables into her dustpan. Owen ran to the end of the row, pulling his squeaky bucket with him. I followed Summer, sponging the tables she had cleared, but I kept my distance. This was already the worst trouble I'd ever been in. No good could come of challenging Owen to a cleaning race, and I knew it.

Max wiped down the benches while I wiped the tables. He brought along a dishpan of soapy water for rinsing the sponges.

Mrs. Wolfowitz called Mr. Allen and Mrs. Novotny on the intercom and told them we'd be late coming back to class. "That's right, Mr. Allen," she said, nodding. "Owen, Max, Nadine, and the new girl."

She went into the kitchen area and sat down on a stool. Mr. Jacobs, the cook, handed her a mug of coffee. I wondered for a minute why Mr. Jacobs, who had a total of maybe six hairs, wore a hairnet every day. Then I went back to sponging. There'd be plenty of time to ponder this and other lunchroom mysteries if getting in this kind of trouble meant my noon meetings at the *Springville Spark* were over.

How much trouble will I be in because of this? I worried. *What if someone else gets to take over my job on the* Spark? Mr. Allen had already mentioned to me that Gordon was interested in being art editor. I didn't want to give up my job on the magazine, but even more important, I didn't want to give up our lunchtime meetings, the only time in the whole school day when I could just be normal with Nick.

All Gordon ever wanted to draw were robots anyway. What kind of a magazine would that be? I squeezed the sponge into the dishpan. The water had turned greenish brown, and now it gave off a moldy kind of smell. I thought I might throw up, but I held my breath and kept wiping.

After a few rows my arms and shoulders ached from scrubbing, so I stretched and looked around. Summer had almost finished clearing off the tables and was already sweeping up the trash piles on the floor. The bigger boy from Mrs. Novotny's class was following her with the trash barrel, and the boy with the broom was working his way down the rows, sweeping steadily to make way for Owen and his mop.

When I bent back to my scrubbing, I thought I saw a flicker of movement out of the corner of my eye—a quick, sneaky kind of motion. But when I looked over, all I saw was Owen, mopping the floor. He didn't seem to be racing Summer at all. For some reason that gave me a bad feeling in the bottom of my stomach.

I kept checking on Owen, but he always just seemed to be concentrating on his job. Then I caught him. I saw him quickly scoop a pile of stuff from a trash can and dump it on the floor. He was making more messes for Summer to pick up. I heard Mrs. Wolfowitz and Mr. Jacobs laughing in the kitchen. I had to get Owen to stop before things got too out of hand. I mean, how much more trouble did he want us all to get into?

"Owen," I hissed.

Too late. Summer had seen him, too. She grabbed her dustpan and whisk broom and made a beeline for Owen. Now he was dumping trash piles as he went, dragging his bucket along with him and slopping water everywhere. This could only end in disaster. I shook my head. I waved my sponge. But I might as well have been invisible. They were on a collision course and the crash point was me. Max and the other two boys just stood there and watched Summer and Owen close in.

Owen veered around the end of my row carrying a handful of trash to dump somewhere. Summer raced toward him from the other end of the row, holding the dustpan in front of her. I dropped my sponge and held my hands out to keep them apart.

"Yah!" Owen shouted. He shoved the mop and bucket at Summer. It rolled past me and I grabbed for the mop handle. The bucket skidded over with a sickening crash. Gray-green water streamed across the floor and slopped over the feet of Mrs. Wolfowitz, who had reappeared on the scene with enormously bad timing.

The lunch lady looked down at her shoes. Then she looked long and hard at me. I was still holding the mop.

4

TWO THOUSAND POUNDS OF ROCKS

B ack to class!" Mrs. Wolfowitz sputtered. Not one of us needed to be told twice. Owen was out the door in a blink. Max dropped his sponge and lit out after him, with the two boys from Novotny's class on his heels. Summer set the dustpan and broom on a table and breezed out. I quickly righted the bucket, shoved the mop in its wringer, and turned to go.

"Not you."

I stopped where I was. Everyone else was already out the door, so Mrs. Wolfowitz had to be talking to me. *Okay,* I thought. *I get it now. This is one of those never-ending nightmares—like when you can't find your homework and you're late for school and you're wading through quicksand and your mother is about to tell you something awful. And even after you wake up it feels like you're trying to breathe with two thousand pounds of rocks on your chest.*

This was just like that.

Mrs. Wolfowitz ordered me to clear away all the trash piles and mop up the dirty water on the floor. Then she stalked over to the far side of the room and buzzed the intercom.

"Yes, Mr. Allen." She raised her voice. "I said Nadine Rostraver."

I knew Mr. Allen would never believe that I'd made all this trouble, no matter what the lunch lady told him. He just couldn't.

It took a really long time to clean up the mess. I didn't think I'd make it home for supper. Or tomorrow's breakfast. I kept my eyes wide open in case any tears tried to get themselves started. I pretended that the mop was a brush and that the floor was a gigantic canvas. At first the mop went *swish*, *swish* in big, angry arcs. Then I concentrated on making smaller and smaller swipes, pretending to fill in the lunchroom floor with a mop painting of the woods at the end of my street. By focusing on my floor painting, I managed to get the rocks on my chest down to maybe one thousand pounds.

By the time I made it back to class, free time was over. In fact, last period was nearly over. I stood outside the classroom door. Would Mr. Allen have to tell my parents what had happened? Thinking of that made those rocks get heavier again.

I could see through the little window in the door that Summer wasn't in the classroom. That seemed fair. First she'd sat me on the boys' side of the lunchroom, and then she'd trapped me in the middle of her stupid race with Owen. Maybe *she'd* disappeared.

Owen was there, shoving papers into his backpack. Nick was copying homework from the board. I turned the doorknob slowly and sidled in.

"Affir-ma-tive," I heard Gordon say to Mr. Allen. "I-will-accept-the-assignment." He nodded several times, chin up chin down. He tilted his head toward his desk and moved one arm and one leg, then the other arm and the other leg. He stopped, tilted his head the other way, and started the whole process again. *Great*, I thought. *Am I being replaced as the* Spark *art director by a robot?*

I flopped into my seat.

"Why'd you go and sit on the boys' side?" Lacey whispered.

I huffed. It wasn't like I'd done it on purpose. Now she was going to act like I was contaminated or something.

Max walked by and kicked the leg of Lacey's chair. "Quit it," Lacey complained. It was hard to believe that last year they used to get along.

I opened the lid of my desk. Inside was a note from Nick. "What happened??" it said.

Summer Crawford, I said to myself. *That's what happened.* I slammed my desk and didn't look at Nick or anyone else. I copied the homework and dug around for my science lab notebook and my math book. At the bottom of the desk was the folder of edited submissions for this week's *Springville Spark.* I'd already sketched out illustrations for some of the stories. No way was I letting Gordon get his mechanical fingers on those. Nick and I could do the layout at home on my computer. I was going to make this issue the best ever so Mr. Allen would beg me to take my old job back. Actually, now that I thought about it, he might not have been talking to Gordon about being art director at all. Maybe Mr. Allen had suggested that Gordon try drawing something besides robots for a change, before his drawing parts wore out.

The last bell rang. I shoved the *Spark* folder into my backpack.

"Have an active and inventive weekend, fellow learners," Mr. Allen said. I had to smile a little. At the end of every week our teacher came up with a new way to say "Don't sit all weekend with your eyes plastered to the tube and video games." Then he turned toward me. "Nadie, may I speak with you for a moment?"

I felt like a soda that had lost its fizz. He moved some papers around, and I knew he was waiting for the rest of the kids to leave. I waited, too.

Mr. Allen's eyebrows were raised in sharp, upside-down Vs. "I must say, Nadie, that I am surprised at and quite disappointed in your behavior today."

"But...but I—"

Mr. Allen held up his hand. "I counted on you to set the very best example for Summer on her first day here at Upper Springville Elementary. Instead, you put yourself in the center of a lunchroom brouhaha."

Brew-ha-what? Any other day the word would have made me laugh, but nothing seemed funny to me right then. How could Mr. Allen think I'd caused all that trouble? He wouldn't even let me tell my side of it. It was so unfair! Right then I would've liked to point out that it was MR. ALLEN who'd put Summer Crawford's desk in our group with Owen, and MR. ALLEN who'd cancelled our lunch meeting so I had to go to the zoofeteria, and MR. ALLEN who'd made me sit with Summer on the boys' side.

"Mrs. Wolfowitz tells me you have additional cafeteria responsibilities during recess on Monday and Tuesday. As you know, Nadie, Monday and Tuesday are the days we edit new *Spark* submissions—"

"But I can still meet at lunch," I broke in.

Mr. Allen shook his head. "No, Nadie. I've already spoken to Gordon about next week's issue. He's been wanting to try his hand at art editing for some time now. I think he deserves a chance, don't you?"

24

I most certainly did not.

"Nadie." Mr. Allen's voice softened. "Everyone slips up now and then. Part of growing up is learning to deal with the consequences of our mistakes."

Just how, exactly, had I "slipped up"? How was any of this my mistake? I had to mop the floor again next week—and I'd lost my art editor job—all because Summer Crawford had set Owen off like a spark to the fuse on a stick of dynamite. All I wanted was the *Springville Spark*, not Summer's troublemaking kind of sparks. Getting blamed for something you didn't do was part of growing up? My eyes stung like needles and I had to get out of there, fast.

"And since we didn't get to finish this week's magazine lay-out—"

"I'm going to do it at home."

"All right," Mr. Allen said. "I'll tell the office that you'll e-mail it in and they can print it first thing Monday morning."

I ran for the door. He hadn't said anything about telling my parents about the lunchroom, and I wasn't going to give him the chance.

* * *

It had stopped sleeting. The thin spring sunlight struggled to warm me through my fleece jacket. Nick was waiting for me at our corner, same as every day since the second day of school this year. The first day of fourth grade had been the day that everything had changed. We'd left school together like we'd done every day of every other year at Springville Elementary, except this time we'd walked out the door of the upper school building. A horde of fifth graders thundered past us, and Nick grabbed the strap of my backpack to pull me out of the way.

"Oooh. Is that your girlfriend?" a fifth grader yelled at Nick.

"Why don't you hold hands instead of backpacks?" another kid jeered.

"Leave them alone—they're probably heading out behind the backstop for privacy."

"Gross me out!"

That was Owen. Some of the other kids in our class said HA HA HA really loud, like they'd always been in with the fifth graders and their great jokes. Nick and I got the "joke," too. Nick let go of my pack strap like it was a snake with poison fangs. The fifth graders jostled in between us and swept us the rest of the way down the steps. Nick and I didn't even look at each other. I walked toward home, and Nick went the other way. The long way. New school, new rules. In Upper Springville Elementary, boys and girls aren't friends.

So now we always left school separately. We walked in opposite directions, then cut back in to meet at the corner of Broom and Laurel. Today, of course, Nick had left school long before me. I stomped past him at the corner and he fell into step beside me.

"Why wasn't Summer in class at the end of the day?" I asked him. "Did they beam her back to wherever she came from?"

"No." Nick shook his head. The way he could never be sarcastic was usually one of the things I liked about Nick. "She had to go to the nurse to read the eye chart."

That figured. Well, my plan was just to ignore her on Monday. Nick didn't say anything, and we kept walking.

"I hate getting into trouble!" I yelled.

"Didn't think you'd like it much," Nick agreed.

"Mr. Allen thinks I threw food and jumped out of my seat. He thinks I dumped dirty water all over the lunchroom floor." I felt mad all over again.

"Wow," Nick said, looking impressed. "You did all that?"

I gave him a little shove.

"Right, right," he said. "You didn't. Right."

"But I'm off the *Spark* next week."

"Off the *Spark*? You can't be!" Now Nick got serious. "Who could take your place?"

I swiveled my head toward him, bent my arms at the elbows, and swung one forward and one back.

"Not Gordon!" Nick slapped his forehead. "You're kidding! Is that what he was talking about with Mr. Allen? The magazine'll be all about robots. But," Nick said, rubbing his head, "you know, he *is* good at computers—"

"Nick!" He hopped ahead of me before I could give him another shove. "Listen," I said, running up to him. "No one is taking my place. At least not permanently." I told him my plan to impress Mr. Allen. "We're going to put together our best issue ever over the weekend. He said I can e-mail the file to school and the office will print it Monday morning."

"That could work," Nick said. "You'll have to stay out of trouble after that, though."

"That's easy," I said. We turned onto our street, Bramble Way. "All I have to do is stay away from Summer Crawford."

5

A MAZE OF
CHALK MARKS

"Hey ho, buddy-pals," my dad said, wiping his hands on a dish towel. The kitchen was full of the smells and mess of baking. A plate piled high with oatmeal raisin cookies sat on the counter. "Perfectly shaped and not a burned one in the batch," Dad said. "These cookies are so beautiful I was about to take them downstairs to the studio to shoot."

"No!" Nick said. "Don't shoot!" He swiped a cookie and stuffed it into his mouth.

I got us milk—regular for me and chocolate soy for Nick. When we started fourth grade, Nick's parents told him he could stay home alone in the afternoons, but none of us wanted to fool around with a routine that had been working great since kindergarten. So Nick still hung out at our house every day until his parents closed their grocery at dinnertime.

Dad reached for the plate.

I pulled it closer to me and covered it with my arms. "Why don't you go pick on fruit or something and leave these poor cookies alone?" For weeks my dad had been photographing covers and spreads for the magazine *You'll Cook It Quick!* He called it *You Can't Cook Zip* because the recipes were totally impossible to follow.

"Pick on fruit or something? That shows what you know," Dad said. He plucked two cookies from the plate, held them up to the window, and turned them in the light. "You'll never guess what I worked on today."

"Kumquats?" I offered.

"Not even close," Dad said.

"What's a kumquat?" Nick asked me. I nudged him with my shoulder. That, of course, wasn't the point.

My dad put the cookies back on the plate and disappeared into the living room. He came back and thunked a big sports bag down on the table.

"What's all that?" I reached for the bag.

"Wait." Dad grabbed the sports duffel away and looked under the table. "Holy moly, Nicolo! When did your tootsies grow into flippers?" He rummaged in the bag. "I hope these'll fit!"

Dad pulled two pairs of inline skates out of the bag. He handed the big yellow ones to Nick and a smaller orange pair to me. "I was doing a shoot for *Outdoor Fun* magazine featuring gear from a super-hot new sports company, and they let me have these."

"Wow!" Nick said. He hugged the skates to his chest. "These are so cool!"

"Thanks, Dad." I held up one of the inline skates. Its four wheels looked kind of skinny to me. "Do you think it matters that neither one of us has ever been on these things before in our lives?" I asked him.

"Yes," Dad said. "That's why I also got all of this." He set aside two extra pairs of skates, then turned the bag upside down. A shower of packages fell onto the table. "Knee pads, elbow pads, wrist guards, you name it. You'll need your bike helmets. They tell me these babies have good brakes once you learn how to use them, but for now I think you'd better stick to flat surfaces."

"We will," Nick said.

"Well, we'll try," I joked.

Before it was Laurel Estates—or "the Shrubs," as we called it—our development had been acres and acres of cornfields. You had to go pretty far before you hit a real hill around here. Our street, Bramble Way, ended in a cul-de-sac, and the lots at the end had never been sold. Beyond the curb, the lots hadn't even been cleared. Tall weeds led the way into the tangle of woods beyond.

I eyed the pile of crash pads Dad had dumped on the table. "Hey, Nick," I said. "Let's get some chalk and draw a skating course on the cul-de-sac. Want to?"

"Yeah!" He ran his hand along the wheels of one of his skates, making them spin. "But first I want to try these on."

"I'm going to pick up Zack from preschool," Dad said. "He started his day extra early this morning, so I think he's going to need a nap. You guys can try the skates at our end of the street while I'm gone if you promise to stay there."

* * *

I grabbed our big bucket of sidewalk chalk and headed out to the cul-de-sac. I didn't even notice Dad drive away. Nick ran home to get his helmet, then came back and sat down at the curb to put on his skates. I started laying out our skating course. I had an idea for a kind of town with winding streets, bridges, and rivers.

"Nadiiiiieee!"

When I looked up, Nick was rolling away. With all of those pads on, he reminded me of one of Gordon's robots. He grabbed at the air as he teetered forward and back.

I dropped my chalk and ran after him. "I'm going to get your hand!" I yelled. "Stop flailing!" When I caught him, he whipped around me in a circle. One of his skates kicked out from under him, then the other one, *flippety-flippety*. But I held Nick's arm up high and he didn't fall.

"There!" Nick huffed. "Stopping's not so hard."

"Not when it's a two-person operation," I observed.

"Let me try again."

I let go and he rolled off again, still a little wobbly. I jogged alongside. "Need help?"

"No," he said. He was heading straight for the curb.

"Nick, here!" I ran next to him with my hand out.

He didn't take it. I held my breath. He hopped the curb and ran a few shaky steps in the weeds, then stopped just in time to avoid the tangle of brambles on the edge of the woods. He turned and smiled. "How was that?"

"Not bad. I'm not sure I'd try it at high speed, though."

"Aren't you going to skate?"

If all-sports Nick was having this much trouble on the skates, I figured I'd be hopeless. "I want to get all of my ideas down before I forget my plan," I told him.

Dad drove up and carried a sleeping Zack into the house. Nick went back to skating and I went back to my chalk. I could hear the *rhurr-rhurr* of his wheels against the pavement as I worked. A couple of times he zipped by so close he almost knocked over the chalk bucket. "Hey!" I called. "Watch where you're going."

He skated around the circle faster and faster. After a while he barreled over to see what I was doing and I had to jump out of the way.

"Quit running me over," I told him.

"I'm getting better, watch!" Nick skated away, then skated toward me. He leaned back on one heel, slowing to a stop right in front of me. He didn't even have to wave his arms much.

"You used the brakes—no more curb!" I was impressed.

"Come on, put your skates on. It's really fun."

"I will in a minute. I just want to finish this street."

"I want to try your skate course," Nick said. "It's looking good."

I watched him skate along one of the paths I'd drawn. The turn was a little too sharp, and he couldn't make it. "I can fix that," I said.

"That's okay. I'll fix it." Nick sat down and took off his skates and helmet. He got some chalk and started adding more roads. I drew in some houses.

"Cool!" Nick looked over my shoulder. "This is turning into a whole little town, right at the end of our street."

The light was fading behind the trees. I could hardly see to draw. I stood up and surveyed the cul-de-sac, which didn't feel so empty anymore. "We should give it a name," I said.

Nick looked out at the winding maze of chalk marks. He rubbed his head. "What about Skatetown?"

"Hmmm." I thought for a second. "I like it, but that could be anywhere. We need something more specific. What about 'Little Shrubs'?" But that didn't sound right either.

"Well, our street is called Bramble Way—and there sure are plenty of brambles around the cul-de-sac," he said.

"Brambleville? Like Springville? No, wait—let's call it Brambletown."

A beam of headlights swung over us. Nick's parents' car pulled into his driveway and the doors slammed.

"Hallo, Nadie!" Mr. Fanelli waved as he went into their house. "Nick! Come help your mama with the bags."

Nick and I grabbed our things and ran to meet Mrs. Fanelli.

"What's for supper?" I asked her.

"Eggplant parmigiana." Nick's mom waved a paper bag under my nose. "This one is yours."

"Mmmm!" I took the bag. "Thanks!" Eggplant parmigiana from the Fanellis' store was my favorite.

"Now, Nadie, you don't forget to leave some for your poor mama," Mrs. Fanelli warned me. "For when she comes home so tired and hungry in the middle of the night."

It would cause Mrs. Fanelli actual physical pain to know that Mom microwaved frozen dinners while she was at work. Dad and I had a pact never to let on about that. Anyway, Mom would be glad we were eating the eggplant—I'd mention it when I instant-messaged her later, like I always did.

A long time ago Dad had tried to tell Mrs. Fanelli that she didn't need to "pay" us with dinner to have Nick over in the afternoons, but she had just waved her hand in the air.

"Tuh!" she'd said, like he was talking nonsense. And that was the end of it. She'd been in charge of her five brothers and two sisters in Italy after their parents had died. That was before she'd met Nick's dad and moved to America.

But she was in charge here, too. No one argued with Mrs. Fanelli.

6

THE PERFECT SPARK

I set another section of track on Zack's train table. "Time to see Mama?" he asked me again. "Not yet, Zacky," I said. "It's only nine thirty and we have to let Mama have her catch-up sleep."

"I don't like ketchup." Zack wrinkled his round nose.

I laughed. I knew he didn't like either one—not the gooey red tomato stuff, and certainly not letting Mom sleep a little later on weekends.

"Nadie! Don't laugh!"

"Sorry." I tickled him under his chin. "Don't laugh," I teased. He squirmed away from my fingers. "How about seeing if your engine can pull the train over this long bridge?"

"My engine is strong!" Zack pushed his wooden train toward the bridge with his pudgy hands. I was building him a complicated track layout, trying to stall him until it was time to wake Mom at ten. I liked the way the toy track could weave back over itself in big loopy designs. I was going to have to show this to Nick for Brambletown.

The steady drizzle outside made the day feel wintery raw. Why had they named this town Springville if we were going to have April days like this one? The bad weather meant no Brambletown today, but that was okay. It was just the right kind of day to work on my dazzling issue of the *Springville Spark*. I planned to spend plenty of time on it, too. I'd show Mr. Allen that no one could do the art editor job the way I did it.

"I'm done with the computer, Nadie," Dad called up from his studio in the basement.

"I want to play computer," Zack said. He pushed himself to his feet, knocking over the bridge.

I looked at the clock. Nine forty-nine. Close enough. "Time to get Mama," I said.

"Mama!" He bolted for my parents' bedroom. I heard the springs creak as he flung himself onto the bed. When I got to the door, he had already burrowed under the blankets. Mom's wavy hair trailed loose across the pillow and the outlines of her face looked soft. She turned over and held her arms out.

"Where's my vitamin N?" She smiled with her eyes closed.

"Only a small dose for now," I said, slipping in and out of her strong hug. "I have to finish up last week's *Springville Spark*." A little part of me wanted to climb into that warm bed with Mom and Zack and let everything that had happened yesterday spill out. But the rest of me was too busy thinking of how to make sure this issue of the *Spark* wouldn't be my last.

* * *

I signed in to our homework connection page and transferred the folder for this week's issue to the desktop. *The Springville Spark*'s "Life in Space!" There were six poems, three articles, a story by Jess, and one by Max. We'd chosen three of Gordon's robot drawings after Mr. Allen had suggested he make at least one robot doing something un-robotlike. Lacey had submitted a drawing of flowers blooming on the moon, tended by moon beings dressed in flowing robes. Alima had painted a cool spiral of light and dark colors that was supposed to be the Big Bang.

An instant message popped up. It was from Nick.

Are you working on the Spark?

Just got started, I typed. I hit Send. *Why don't you come over?* I added. I hit Send again. I counted to twenty. Nothing. I counted another twenty, then heard steps outside on the walk. Upstairs, the kitchen door slammed. *Ba-bump, ba-bump, ba-bump,* Nick thumped down to our basement.

He shrugged out of his raincoat and draped it over a chair. You didn't need a raincoat to run across the street, but no one argued with Mrs. Fanelli.

"What took you so long?" I asked.

He held on to the arms of the chair and let himself down slowly. "I'm sore," he groaned.

I laughed. "Guess I'd better stay off of those skates."

"Nah—it's worth it," Nick insisted. He pulled his chair closer. "You have to get on those skates so we can start practicing on our course."

"We have to finish drawing it first," I said.

"You mean start again." Nick pointed to the drops splashing against the high basement window. "The rain's washing the chalk away."

"Oh," I sighed. "Right. Well, we have something more important to do today, anyway."

I showed him the files on the computer screen. We inserted them into a publishing document and tried different ways of fitting them into our four-page layout. After we fixed on a layout, Nick played around with fancy fonts and came up with some good ones for the titles. Using my dad's computer stylus and drawing tablet, I added illustrations for the stories and articles. I worked slowly and carefully, making border art for each page with repeat patterns of planets and stars. Feeling generous, I made one of Gordon's robots small and put it in the pattern, too.

"Nice touch," Nick observed. "I'm glad you thought of taking those border planets and stuff from the diagrams in our science lab packet."

"Do you think this is the best issue we've ever done?" I asked, frowning at the screen. "It has to be the best ever." I pulled the stylus out of my mouth and tried to rub off my teeth marks.

"I think it looks great," Nick said. "I really like your drawing of the astronaut walking on the moon." He was jotting down notes for his editor's column. "These borders and titles go way quicker on your dad's computer than on the one at school."

"Yeah, and especially without Mr. Allen getting in the way." Now that I thought about it, I was almost madder at Mr. Allen for assuming I'd been the lunchroom troublemaker than I was at Summer for starting all the trouble. Nick didn't say anything.

"Come on," I prodded, "you know Mr. Allen's hopeless at computer layout stuff."

"Well, he *is* a really good editor," Nick said. "He shows us how to make the writing stronger and helps us decide what the stories are really about. And he's great at suggesting which ones go together in an issue."

I pursed my lips and started sketching for the cover. I wasn't interested in hearing about our teacher's good points. Now, if Nick wanted to talk about Mr. Allen's pointy eyebrows or his ridiculous purple sneakers, that might be different. In the middle of the page I drew a big Earth and the moon orbiting around it. I added the International Space Station and a couple of other satellites. On my computer screen, the Milky Way and other planets with their moons and rings took shape in the distance. I washed in deep blues, blue-greens, yellows, and bits of red. The cover was the only illustration in the *Spark* that could be in color, so it had to be spectacular.

I closed my eyes and rolled my chair away from the computer. Then I turned back and squinted at the image on the screen. I liked the overall effect, but something was missing. Nick looked up from his writing.

"What do you think?" I asked him.

He rubbed his chin. He tilted his head and squinted.

"Out with it, Fanelli."

"It needs something," he ventured.

"Yeah, yeah," I said. "But what?"

Nick and I both stared at the cover of the *Springville Spark*'s "Life in Space!" issue. "Some kind of connection to our class, maybe?" he said.

A picture jumped into my head. "Yes! That's it!" I scooted my chair back to the stylus tablet. Hah! I'd show Mr. Allen— I'd send him into outer space! That's where he belonged anyway, if he could possibly believe that I'd caused all the trouble in the zoofeteria. My stylus raced around the drawing tablet. Nick bent his head over his notebook. I put the final touches on my artwork and as soon as I was finished, I quickly switched to the editor's page.

"Wait!" Nick protested. "I didn't see it yet."

"Let's put your column in first." I wanted to keep the suspense going.

"Okay." Nick pulled his chair over to the keyboard and typed in his column. Then he moved back. He drummed a happy two-fingered rhythm on his knee while I read.

Who's Out There?

One of the most interesting questions we asked during our study of the solar system is if life exists in other parts of space. Can we really be the only ones? It's fun to think about other forms of life out there—where they might be and what they might be like. Contacting them would be exciting. It would change everything! If beings from outer space came to Earth, would we try to understand them? Would we show respect for them? That is what we have to work on.

Nick Fanelli, editor

I raised one eyebrow at him.

"What?" he protested, his eyes too wide open. Another really great thing about Nick was that he was just no good at lying.

"Oh, nothing, Nick." *Fine*, I thought. *If he's going to pretend his column isn't about getting along with Summer Crawford, then I can pretend I don't get it.* I moved Lacey's drawing of moon flowers and moon beings next to his editorial. Then I switched back to my cover art.

Nick studied the screen. He grinned. "Nice," he said, nodding. "Mr. Allen looks great in that picture. Good move. A total job-getter-backer."

I folded my arms. "All it needs is a more exciting title. I'll think about that later. Do you want me to show it to you before I e-mail it in?" I hit the Save button.

"Nah," Nick said. "If it goes along with that drawing, it'll be perfect!"

7

CONTACT

Sunday broke blue-sky bright and dry. Our house had its delicious Sunday morning coffee smell, with a hint of cinnamon today.

"Want to come to the park with Zack and me?" Dad asked.

"Swing and slide!" shouted Zack.

Dad shifted his camera to one side and tucked my wiggly brother under his other arm. He was waiting for my answer.

I thought for a minute. Mom was still asleep, and Nick was at church. This would be the perfect time to try out those skates without anybody seeing how uncoordinated I was.

"No thanks," I told him. "I'm going to stay here and skate."

"Okay, but don't forget," Dad said. "Pads—"

"Pads, helmet, flat ground," I recited.

"Always the perfect student," Dad laughed. He shifted his grip on Zack and went out the door.

To everyone but Mr. Allen, I thought. Then I remembered the *Spark* I'd just e-mailed to the school office. I smiled a little. Mr. Allen was sure to change his mind about me after he saw that.

I sat on our front steps and pulled my hair into a ponytail. I put on the knee pads, then the elbow pads and the wrist guards. I had to shove hard to get my feet into the inline skates. My bike helmet was the only thing that felt normal. How was I supposed to actually move with all the rest of this stuff on? I glanced over at Brambletown—or where Brambletown used to be. It had all washed away in the rain. The street was completely dry now, though. Nick and I could draw it again, maybe this afternoon. I figured I'd have an even better idea of how to lay it out after skating around for a while.

I tried to push to my feet. The skates were stiff and clunky. And slippy-tippy. After a lot of unsuccessful starts, I teetered upright. The wrist guards pressed into my hands. I wobbled away from the house and tripped over the crack where the driveway met the street. I went down hard. No wonder Nick was sore.

I was never so glad that Nick's house and mine were the only ones at our end of the street. When I finally managed to get myself back up again, my toes were pointing toward the corner, not the cul-de-sac. I decided to skate a few yards in that direction, just to get the feel of it, then turn around and skate back. On the first step my left skate hit a pebble and I tripped forward, landing on my hands and knees again. My knees throbbed right through the pads. Next time up, I tried to make more of a gliding motion with the skates. The wheels started to roll faster, helped by the cool breeze pushing at my back. I scoured the street just in front of me and skipped my feet sideways when I saw rocks.

At the corner I kept my skates together and leaned to the left, trying to make a U-turn so I could double back to my house. But I couldn't make my turn sharp enough for a U. All I managed was a left turn onto Bayberry Street. *No problem*, I thought. Bayberry was perfectly level, just like Bramble Way. I knew I should probably move to the sidewalk, but I wasn't sure I could make it up one of the driveways. Anyway, looking at all those sidewalk cracks convinced me that the street would be a lot safer for my aching knees.

Trying not to lose my balance, I looked both ways. I didn't see a car in either direction. Sunday mornings were always quiet in the Shrubs.

I worked at trying to find a rhythm—push and glide, push and glide—and stayed as close to the curb as I could without bumping my skate against it. My legs were still wobbling, but I'd straightened up a bit. I still kept a close eye out for pebbles and sticks. Forget about trying to stop. My knees couldn't take another fall.

I veered wide at the corners and looked both ways when I crossed the empty intersections. I was concentrating so hard I didn't hear the car come up behind me. HONK! I jumped and my feet kicked out from underneath me. I windmilled my arms, trying not to fall backward.

When I caught my balance, I realized I wasn't in the Shrubs anymore. I passed the back of our school, moving faster than I wanted to. I had never noticed that some of the roads sloped ever so slightly downhill away from our street. Why hadn't I thought to practice stopping before I left my driveway?

The streets on the other side of the school were even less familiar to me and there were more cars. I thought I'd better try and go back. I made a right turn, and then another, but I didn't recognize the names of the streets. One of them should have been the way back to the Shrubs. It was even hillier in this neighborhood. I rolled faster, I was breathing harder, and my heartbeats pounded in my ears. Now I *really* didn't want to fall. The hill steepened and my arms shot out to the sides, grabbing at air. At this speed I knew I could never jump the curb the way Nick had done.

I hurtled past an old house. *I can't stop!* I thought wildly. I could see the bottom of the hill rushing toward me. The street dead-ended in a tangle of dry scrub without a curb. I headed as far to the left as I could manage, then leaned right, desperately trying to veer into a U-turn. I wasn't going to make it. I threw my arms in front of my face and crashed into the weeds.

I rumbled across the uneven ground, a low *uhhhhnnnnn* coming from deep in my chest. Stickers ripped at my arms and tall weeds whipped my cheeks. The skates rolled me a lot farther than I would have thought possible. Just when I started to wonder if I'd go on bumping through the tangled brush like that forever, the skates got ahead of the rest of me. I landed on my back in the thicket with a *whump* that knocked all my breath right out. I stared up at the blue, blue sky and tried to gulp some air back in.

Then I heard something else crash through the weeds. It came closer and closer. The something else stopped right over me, blotting out the sun. It panted with its mouth hanging open, showing white fangs and a slobbery tongue. Oddly, the thing smelled like cats. A long string of drool dangled from its livery lips. I saw the drool dangle lower and lower until it fell off and landed on my neck. I closed my eyes and shuddered.

Maybe I was knocked out by my fall, I thought hopefully. *Maybe I'm hallucinating.*

I felt a tongue slurp across my face.

"To-by!" A voice called from somewhere in the distance. "Toby!"

More crashes in the weeds.

"Toby! What did you find?" That voice sounded familiar. "Toby, shove over." There was more rustling and some grunting. The panting shifted to the side.

"Nadie? Is that you?"

I opened my eyes. So much for staying away from Summer Crawford.

* * *

"It's good my dog Toby found you," Summer said. "Your cuts don't look too serious, but I don't think these will do it." She put a handful of plastic bandages back into her pocket. "You'd better come with me."

I didn't want to go anywhere with Summer, but I couldn't think what else to do. It was like my brain wasn't working after all of that jiggling. My arms and legs stung. I took off my helmet, wrist guards, and skates, and followed her out of the weeds. We walked up the street and stopped in front of the old house. My feet ached and stickers grabbed at my socks. The black Labrador retriever, Toby, nosed open the gate.

"My mom had to work today," Summer said. "She's the new manager at the paint and wallpaper store and they're doing inventory. My big sister will be back soon."

"Inventory?" I repeated, still suffering from brain-jiggle.

"It's when they count up everything in the store. Sunday's a good day for counting, since they're closed for customers." She opened her front door and motioned for me to go in.

The smell hit me full force. It was that part fishy cat food, part litter box smell I'd noticed on her sweater and on Toby.

Two white cats watched me from the stairs. One had a bandage on its ear. A fat orange cat walked down the hallway. I could see at least three others in the living room, sitting on boxes. Six evil Francis-types and who knew how many more? The hairs on the back of my neck started to prickle.

"I'm okay, Summer, really," I said, backing up. "I should probably just go home."

"Come *on*," she insisted. "Let me fix you up so you don't bleed all over town." She pulled me down the hall into the kitchen and sat me at the round wooden table covered with silverware and a pile of crumpled newspapers. "You can just put your stuff on the floor."

I slowly set down my skates and helmet. A black cat and a Siamese with a wide bare spot on its back stared at me from the counter next to the refrigerator. I kept an eye on them while I pulled out my hair elastic, along with some weed stalks, and fixed my ponytail. A stack of boxes with Hill Street written on them in black Magic Marker leaned against the wall.

"Time to get down," Summer told the cats. She cuddled each of them and put them on the floor. The black one skittered across the room. The Siamese arched its back, took a few steps, then slunk in my direction.

"Don't give her any of this," Summer said, handing me a glass of lemonade. "I'll be right back. I think my first aid stuff's in the basement." She opened a door and disappeared down some steps.

The black cat immediately hopped back up onto the counter and sat facing me. The Siamese slipped under my chair and twisted its body in and out through the legs. I picked up my feet and stopped breathing. It walked a short distance away, then turned and sprang onto the table. I jumped up, knocking over my chair. The back door opened, and an older version of Summer with pink, spiky hair came in. She was wearing headphones.

"Hey!" She swatted the Siamese off the table. "Rats don't drink lemonade!" The cat stalked out of the room. I just stood there. Summer's sister looked at me for a couple of seconds, then shook her head and went upstairs.

I picked up my chair, keeping my eyes fixed on the black cat. When I sat down, the two white cats came into the kitchen. My heart was *thump-thump*ing. There was no way to keep track of all of these cats.

Summer burst back into the room waving an old Sesame Street lunch box. "Got it!" she announced.

I didn't think even Big Bird could help me now.

"I'm always patching up my cats or Toby, so I've got all kinds of good stuff in here." Summer opened the box and took out antiseptic wipes and bandages of every shape and size. She found a pair of tweezers and got to work on the collection of prickers in my arms. She bit her lower lip, concentrating hard.

"This is a lot less gross than when my cats get into stuff," she said. "You should see some of the things they come up with. They could teach Owen a thing or two." She laughed.

I pulled my arm away and looked at Summer. "You know," I told her, "Owen isn't joking around with you. Boys and girls don't joke around much with each other in fourth grade. They don't sit on the same side of the cafeteria. There are rules. Boys and girls aren't friends."

"Oh, you mean like you and Nick, for instance?"

My mouth dropped open.

"I guess some rules are for following, and some aren't," Summer said with a shrug.

Just one big gash in my arm needed bandaging. At home I liked to do my own bandages, but there was no way I could fix myself up and keep watch on all of those cats at the same time. While Summer swabbed my cut, I thought about what she had said about rules.

"Phewf!" she said finally, pushing her hair behind her ears. "There. You're almost as good as before." She snapped the lunch box closed.

"Thanks," I said. "Thanks a lot." Right at that moment I wasn't at all sure how good I'd been before. I'd been blaming Summer for everything that had happened. But deep down I knew she hadn't tried to get me in trouble. And she didn't know about my job for the *Spark* or that I might lose it.

As she swung the refrigerator door shut, she caught me eyeing the giant turkey carcass on a platter inside. "Want some?" Summer asked. She swung the door open again.

I looked at the places on the turkey where hunks were missing and the full parts that were left. It was funny, how Summer did just whatever she wanted to do, no matter what anyone thought about it.

"Yes," I said.

"Mayo?"

I thought for a minute. "Okay," I said.

* * *

After we put the turkey away, I asked Summer if I could use her phone to let my mom know where I was. I told Mom I'd been out skating and was on my way back.

"Where are you calling from?" Mom asked.

"A friend's house." Summer smiled when I said that, the same shy but open way she had when I'd given her the carrots in the lunchroom on Friday. I smiled, too.

"Okay, then," Summer said when I hung up. "Let's get going." She headed out the back door and went into the garage. In a few seconds she came out wheeling a rickety old bike. One of those kiddie trailers, like a little tent on wheels, was hooked onto the back.

"Good thing you're you, Nadie," she said. "You're probably just at the weight limit for this thing. We'll have to walk it up the hill, though. Then you can get in."

Summer held one handlebar and I held the other and together we pushed the bike up the street. I carried my skates. The pavement felt cold through my socks. At the top, she pointed to the blue and yellow trailer.

"Better sit right in the middle," she said. "You can move the blanket if you want."

I climbed in and set my skates on one side.

"Contact!" Summer yelled.

The big orange cat bounded out of the house, ran up the street, and leaped into the trailer right next to me.

"Contact loves to come for rides," Summer told me. "Don't worry, she won't hop out or anything." Contact's hopping out wasn't even on the same planet as my worries. Summer started pedaling.

The orange cat looked me over. She put out her paw and

swatted my thigh. I gulped. She swatted me with her other paw.

"Don't let Contact bother you," Summer called over her shoulder. "She thinks she should get all of the room just because she's having kittens."

Great, I thought. *I get through all of this and now I'm going to get slashed to death by a pregnant orange version of Francis.*

Then Contact leaped right into my lap.

"Eep!" I squeaked.

Summer didn't hear me. Contact prodded my legs with the pads of her paws, turned around in two circles, and curled up in my lap. It was hard work to sit perfectly still in a moving bike trailer. The cat was big and lumpy, and parts of her shifted as we rode. I felt, more than heard, a noise I'd surely never heard Francis make—a continuous, quiet sort of rumble. I picked up my hand very slowly and ran it along her soft fur. I scratched her behind her crooked orange ears. Contact's noise got louder.

Purring, I decided. *This cat is purring.*

8

ROOM TWENTY, FREEZE!

Zack got so excited telling me about what he was going to play at preschool that he drenched me with his bowl of Banana-O's the next morning. Nick had to go on ahead to school while I changed my clothes. I hoped Mr. Allen wouldn't say anything about our issue of the *Spark* before I got there. I wanted to hear every word of his rave review firsthand.

Nick and I had talked about our issue of the class magazine for hours on Sunday afternoon while we chalked new and better roads for Brambletown. We couldn't wait to see Mr. Allen's face when he saw the cover, and the editorial, too.

"He's going to be impressed," I'd ventured.

"He's going to be amazed! Poor Gordon. Mr. Allen will probably put you back in charge right away."

But I knew Nick's last comment had probably been a bit optimistic, since there was still the little matter of me mopping the lunchroom floor during today's editorial meeting, and Tuesday's, too.

I got to school in record time. On my way into the building, I picked up my copy of the *Spark* from the pile next to the office door. I smiled down to my toes. If I had to say so myself, the cover was a masterpiece. The solar system stood out against a beautiful blue-green wash. And there in the center was our teacher holding up the Earth on an open science book, like he was giving it to us on a platter. Just in case any-one was too dense to get it, I'd changed the title to *The Springville Spark: Mr. Allen Brings New Life to the Solar System!*

I strode into the classroom and risked a quick grin at Nick. But he was slumped in his seat staring straight ahead, his chin on his fists.

Although Mr. Allen wasn't in the room, lots of other kids were sitting at their desks, writing or drawing something. That was normal for Gordon, but not for everybody else. I had expected the classroom to be buzzing about the new *Spark* issue.

Jess and Alima had their heads together, and they were gig-gling like mad. I peered over their shoulders. I didn't get it.

They were making changes to my drawing of Mr. Allen, and the changes were not at all complimentary. Mr. Allen now had what looked like four green trumpets coming out of his head. His eyebrows stretched up over his head in big black points, and his sneakers had turned into giant purple paws.

"Why are you wrecking it?" I cried.

"What?" Alima looked at me like *I* was the one doing something stupid. At the next table, Max's *Spark* cover was a different version of the same horrible joke. So was everyone else's in his group, except Gordon's. Oddly, Gordon seemed to be the only person *not* drawing that morning besides Nick. I ran to the next group, and then to mine. Lacey was just finish-ing her cover.

"How could you?" I yelled at her.

"I'm just going along with the joke," she said. She tugged on her bangs, looking a little confused.

I turned to Nick. "Why aren't you doing anything? They're ruining all our work!"

He folded his arms across his chest and stared straight through me like I wasn't even there.

I heard a scraping sound from the back of the room. Owen had dragged over a chair, and he was pinning his own messy masterpiece high on the bulletin board. Some other kids raced back and handed theirs up to him.

"Stop it!" I shouted. "Don't!" I ran over to the bulletin board. Owen hopped down and knocked the chair away. I jumped up as high as I could, but I couldn't reach those pictures. I grabbed for the chair. Owen pulled it back in a crazy tug-of-war. Kids ran toward us. Desks crashed and books toppled.

"ROOM TWENTY, FREEZE!"

We froze. One of the ruined *Spark* covers detached from the bulletin board and floated gently down like a falling leaf. I snatched it out of the air and stuffed it in my pocket.

"Return to your seats," said Mr. Allen sternly. "This behavior is extremely disappointing."

We slunk back to our desks. Nick didn't look up. How had everything gone so wrong? I covered my face with my hands.

"Nadie and Nick, I'll see you both out in the hall," our teacher said. "I expect the rest of you to spend the time putting our classroom back in order. In *silence!*"

* * *

"I've just come from Mrs. Winger's office," Mr. Allen began. "Apparently this cover of yours has created quite a sensation in other classrooms as well. There have been many creative additions to the cover, including some very unflattering drawings of other teachers. I must say, Nadie, I would have expected you to come up with something more suitable for this particular issue of the *Spark*. You too, Nick. Satire has its place, but it isn't always appropriate, especially in a school magazine that goes out to younger students, as well as teachers, parents, the principal—"

"S-satire?" I stammered.

"Yes, that was satire. Making fun of something in a sarcastic way."

"But Mr. Allen, it wasn't—"

He held up his hand. "It was a poor choice, and one that wouldn't have been made if we had worked on the issue together as we should have. I take responsibility for that, and I told Mrs. Winger as much. I assured her that I wouldn't let anything like this happen again. If it does, we'll lose the privilege of publishing our magazine."

I knew that Mr. Allen was speaking to us in his usual exact manner. He was using the English language. So why couldn't I understand a word of what he was saying? Satire? Poor choice? Lose the *Spark*? I felt as if I'd been transported into some kind of weird parallel universe.

Mr. Allen spoke again. "I'd like the two of you to go down to the media center computers and work on a note of explanation and apology to Mrs. Winger. We will go over it together after school. I'm sorry," he added, "but as of now you are *both* relieved of your duties on the *Spark*."

* * *

Nick took off down the hall. He was practically running.

"Nick, wait!"

I caught up with him at the door of the media center and grabbed his arm, but he shook me off and went inside. He sat down at a computer in the far corner. I pulled up a chair and sat beside him.

"Thanks a lot!" Nick's face was flushed. He was really angry.

"Thanks for *what*? What's going on here? We didn't do satire! You *never* do anything sarcastic!"

"But *you* do," Nick shot back. "I can't believe you changed our title to *that*!"

"Shhhh!" A fifth-grade boy at the next computer glared at us.

I leaned in close to Nick. "What do you mean, you can't believe I changed it to *that*?" I hissed. "It's a great title."

"I can't even talk to you," Nick said.

I exploded. "What is going on, Nick? What's wrong with *Mr. Allen Brings New Life to the Solar System*?"

Nick stared at me. "That's not what it says," he said evenly. "And you know it." He clamped his mouth shut in a thin line. He turned away from me and opened a blank file on the computer.

I snatched the crumpled cover out of my pocket and looked at the title. What I saw hit me like a punch in the stomach. My title for the issue didn't say: *Mr. Allen Brings New Life to the Solar System!* It said: *Mr. Alien Brings New Life to the Solar System!*

"But—but I didn't write that," I sputtered. I pulled my chair in closer and tried to calm my shaky voice. "I wrote Mr. *Allen*."

"You were mad at Mr. Allen the whole time we were working on this issue—making fun of him, even. But I can't believe you'd do this to the *Spark*."

"I—I must have typed it wrong. I didn't mean to write 'alien'!"

"Well,"—Nick's ears were bright red—"then you made a really stupid mistake."

That did it. "*You're* the editor!" I shouted. "It's your job to check the issue for mistakes, and you didn't!"

"I would have if you'd showed me the cover before you sent it!"

"Could you take your lovers' quarrel somewhere else?" the fifth grader said with a smirk.

I bumped my chair away from Nick's. "I'm going to write my own note to Mrs. Winger," I told him. "I'm not working with you."

"Fine."

"Fine." I moved to a different computer and glared at the monitor. A skier tumbled down a mountain in a giant snowball screen saver. I knew just how that skier felt.

9

A CHANGE SET
IN MOTION

Have invigorating insect investigations!" Mr. Allen told the class as everyone filed out for the day. Everyone except Nick and me.

Mr. Allen sat down at the computer where Nick was waiting to show him the apology letter to the principal. I dragged my feet and the rest of me over to stand near them.

"Dear Mrs. Winger," Mr. Allen read aloud. He trailed the cursor across Nick's words on the screen. "We're sorry that we typed a stupid mistake on the cover of the *Spark*. It was not supposed to be a bad joke. It was supposed to say Mr. Allen, not Mr. Alien. If we get another chance to work on the *Spark*, the editor will be much more careful to check for stupid mistakes."

Our teacher turned to look at us. "Does this message represent the best effort from both of you?"

"No," I said.

Mr. Allen looked over at Nick, then back at me. The *tick tick tick* of the wall clock echoed in the empty classroom. "You know, the two of you had the best editorial partnership I've ever seen in a school magazine. You are capable of remarkable work together."

I made sure my face didn't move. I watched the cursor blink on and off where Mr. Allen had left it, right on top of the word "stupid."

Stupid magazine, stupid school, stupid friendship.

Mr. Allen cleared his throat. "I've had all day to reflect on this, and I am quite certain that you each had the best intentions for this issue of the *Spark*. A mistake was made, and I apologize for reacting to it so harshly this morning in the heat of the moment. Clearly your exuberant artwork and your editorial about showing understanding to others demonstrate the tone you meant to set."

Right. Nick shows understanding to *others*—to Summer, to outer-space life forms—to everybody but me. Some friend.

"Other students do need a chance to serve on the editorial board at some point," Mr. Allen said. "I'm sorry about the unfortunate circumstances, but a change has been set in motion. I think we'll use this opportunity to let some of your classmates work on the *Spark* for a while, and then at a future date we'll reassess the situation."

Nick was staring at the wall. I shifted from foot to foot.

"Do either of you want to add anything?" Mr. Allen asked.

I shook my head.

"Nope," Nick said.

"All right then. I'll see you both tomorrow." He eyed the computer screen, then turned to us again. "I suppose," he added, "that for now we'll let my apology to Mrs. Winger stand on its own."

Nick and I practically got stuck in the doorway trying to be the first out. We racewalked down the hall and slammed open the double doors, me on the left, Nick on the right. We separated down the steps and stomped off in our opposite directions. When I was sure he could no longer see me, I broke into a run. He wasn't at the corner of Broom and Laurel. I ran the rest of the way home and slammed the kitchen door behind me.

"Aren't you guys a little late?" Dad asked, coming up from his studio. He looked around. "Where's Nick? Getting his skates?" He whisked a plate of something off the counter and set it on the table. "Well, he'd better hurry back. I made his favorite—peach, banana, and peanut butter sandwiches." He hugged me around my shoulders, grabbed the car keys from the hook, and went out the door. "See you guys when I get back with Zack," he called.

"I hate peach, banana, and peanut butter sandwiches," I muttered as Dad drove away. I sat at the table and pushed the sandwich triangles around on the plate. After a while I heard the *rhurr-rhurr* of skate wheels on pavement. From the corner of the window I saw Nick gliding through Brambletown. *It's not fair that he's out there,* I thought. *Brambletown was my idea.*

Nick glanced toward our house and I shrank back against the wall. When I looked again, he was skating straight across the lot, ignoring the chalked roads and crossing over the houses and shops. He went up his driveway, threw his helmet down on the grass, and clomped over to his front steps. He took off his skates and disappeared into his house.

I waited a few minutes, then got my bucket of chalk from the garage and went out to Brambletown. I sat for a while with a piece of chalk in my hand.

"How could one little typing mistake have caused such a mess?" I wailed. It made me ache from the inside out.

Instead of thinking about the *Spark,* I started making lines on the blacktop. The vibration of the chalk against the rough pavement traveled up my arm. The bandage Summer had put there was starting to curl at the edges. *So what if she helped me,* I thought. None of this, NONE of it would have happened if she hadn't come here in the first place.

I examined the set of lines I'd made. They looked like rows of bricks. I filled them in with brown chalk so they looked more like stacks of chocolate bars and added a sign lettered in gumdrop colors for a candy shop. I knew Nick would like the chocolate part. I got halfway up to go and get him, then sat back down. I thought about rubbing the brown bricks away, but I didn't. Dad drove up with Zack.

"I want to draw!" Zack called. He ran down the driveway and barreled into me. He smelled like paste, and a construction paper circle was stuck on his elbow.

"Okay," I told him. I held out a handful of fat pastel chalk. "You pick the color."

He grabbed a piece of chalk and sat down. I watched him make pink squiggles, pink stripes, and pink blobs. I took my own piece of chalk and finished the striped awning of my candy shop. Zack leaned over my shoulder.

"It's a candy shop," I said.

Zack smiled. "I like candy." He bit off a piece of his pink chalk. In Dad's health-food universe, I wondered which was worse, Zack eating candy or Zack eating pink sidewalk chalk.

"Spit that out," I told him.

He clamped his mouth shut.

"Okay, Zacky, let's go show Dad, then." I took him by the hand and hurried him inside.

"Bleah." He stuck his tongue out for Dad to see.

"Uh-oh!" Dad wiped the chalk off of Zack's tongue and handed him a sandwich triangle.

"Is Nick all right?" Dad asked me. He pointed to the plate of sandwiches. "Why isn't he here?"

"Because he lives across the street," I said, concentrating hard on washing my hands at the kitchen sink.

"Oh?" Dad laughed. "Since when?"

"He's in fourth grade, Dad. He doesn't need a babysitter."

I wiped my hands on the dish towel. I could feel Dad watching me. "Something going on?" he asked.

"Yup," I said past the wedge in my throat. "What's going on is I'm going skating."

* * *

I coasted around Brambletown alone. The skate town had seemed like such a great idea. Now just following a bunch of colored lines on the flat lot was boring. Shadows stretched across the chalk roads and my skate hit a pebble, launching me forward onto the pavement. My palms stung. Just in case Nick had seen me fall, I stayed on the ground, pretending to look for something.

A big ant crawled into my line of vision, right across a red and white Brambletown stop sign. I found the pebble I'd tripped on and hurled it into the woods. Now the ant was crawling across the letter P in STOP. Watching that ant reminded me about my science homework. We were supposed to collect a bug and bring it in tomorrow for the new unit, *Insects and How They Eat*. Mr. Allen had raved on and on about how much fun this assignment would be. But after today, I wasn't in the mood for Mr. Allen's kind of fun.

Some ants bite, so I wasn't about to pick up that big one with my bare fingers. I skated up to my house, changed into my sneakers, and dug around in my backpack for the little plastic vial Mr. Allen had passed out to each of us. By the time I got back to Brambletown, the ant was gone. I didn't bother to look for it. I figured I could find something better anyway. I'd show Nick and Mr. Allen and everyone else by bringing in something really different. Something really cool.

I headed for our garden, but the sun was almost all the way down now. It was getting colder, and I couldn't see much of anything in the deep shadows between the bushes. A couple of times I thought I spotted something crawling in some old dead leaves, but when I looked closer it wasn't there. I shook the branches of the rhododendron, hoping an interesting specimen would drop out. No luck. Dark was seeping into the garden and I still didn't have a bug. I couldn't go to school tomorrow empty-handed after what had happened today. I wondered what kind of bug Nick had found.

I went inside, got a flashlight, and poked around in the flower bed. The dirt had that damp, woody promise of living things just waiting to sprout. I still didn't see a single insect, not even an ant. Finally I turned over a rock like Nick always did when we went into the woods or down to the stream. Nothing but a few pillbugs.

So much for something really cool—anyone could find a pillbug. "Come on, little roly-poly," I sighed. The small oval bug curled into a silver-gray ball as soon as I touched it. I set the rim of the vial on the ground and tapped the pillbug in with my finger. It rolled to the bottom. As I was closing the vial, headlight beams swept across the cul-de-sac, then a car door slammed. Mrs. Fanelli walked across the street carrying the dinner sack, just like always. I crouched down between the rhododendrons.

"I called to check on him," I heard Dad tell Nick's mom. "Neither one is talking." He said something else I couldn't quite hear.

"Don't argue with me, Dan," Mrs. Fanelli said. "Take this dinner right now."

And she marched back across the inky street without her sack.

10
ROOM TWENTY STINKS

I rushed around after breakfast the next morning, searching for something to use for my bug habitat. Mr. Allen had asked us to bring in an empty soda bottle. Why would our teacher assume that we all had soda at home? We didn't. I hoped that Lacey, the junk food queen, would have an extra bottle.

We were also supposed to pay attention to where we'd found the bug and bring in something it might like to eat. Pillbugs lived in dirt, and so did potatoes. Good thing I knew there were still a few left in the bag from when Mom had tried to make that awful potato soufflé recipe she'd found in *You Can't Cook Zip*. It was getting late, so I grabbed the bag from the pantry and shoved it into my backpack on my way out the door.

Wisps of hair stung at my eyes and a chilly wind pushed me along the sidewalk. Part of me was thinking that maybe, if I saw him on the way to school, I'd ask Nick, in a casual kind of way, what bug he'd collected. I had my vial in my hand, ready to show him the pillbug. But I never saw him at all.

* * *

"Leave your food items in your coatroom cubby for now, my entomologist colleagues," Mr. Allen told us. "Please clear your desks of everything but your collecting vial."

Nick was already sitting in his seat. His vial was full of water. Something long and brown was swimming around in there. He saw me looking and turned away. I pretended I'd been looking at Owen's desk, even though Owen wasn't there yet. *Why did Nick collect that swimming thing?* I wondered. *Fish aren't bugs.* I twirled my vial around and around, admiring my pillbug. They might be easy to find, but they were nice in their own way. I liked how they rolled up tight when they needed to protect themselves. Summer had what looked like a dull gray button in her vial. Something fluttered in Lacey's. Owen slid into his seat and hid his bug in his desk before anyone could see what it was.

Mr. Allen rubbed his hands together. "I'm sure we have an exciting variety of insects to study," he said. "I've placed a diagram on each group of desks that explains how to identify what you've found. Let's see how far along in this process we already are. If you know the name of your insect, raise your hand."

Every kid in our group put their hand up, even Owen. In the other groups it seemed to be about half and half.

"Very good!" Mr. Allen smiled. "Let's jump right in and see what Group Two has brought to share with us."

Chairs scraped and squeaked as the rest of the class gathered around our desks.

"I'll go last," Owen said, his vial still inside his desk. He shifted his eyes around the group and settled on Summer.

I knew right then and there that he had brought in something really gross.

Summer smiled at Owen. I felt a chill creep under my skin.

"I'll go first," Lacey announced. "I have a pretty butterfly." She waved her vial in the air. Inside was a small, silvery moth.

"Aha," Mr. Allen said.

"It's a wheat moth," I said. I knew full well it wasn't a butterfly. When Mom finds a wheat moth in our kitchen cabinet she always saves it to show Dad. She says that it came from the whole wheat flour bin at the health food store, and that it proves that health food isn't really good for you after all.

"Moths and butterflies are close relatives," Mr. Allen told us. "Lacey, you'll be able to give us some good information about the similarities and differences. What did you bring, Nick?"

A stupid fish, I thought. *Too bad, Nick, wrong assignment.*

Nick held up his vial. "A hellgrammite." Some of the kids giggled.

"Did you hear that?" Alima whispered loudly. "Nick said H-E-double-L."

Mr. Allen took Nick's vial and whistled. "A real beaut! Now here's the six thousand–point question: What type of creature is a hellgrammite?"

"Fish bait!" Max said. "I use those when I go fishing with my mom. Boy, can they pinch! Where'd you get it?"

"I found it in the stream near my house," Nick said.

It wasn't the stream near *his* house, it was the stream near *my* house. Going to the stream was something Nick and I always did together. He must have sneaked around through the woods behind his house the really long way just so I wouldn't see him. Well, too bad. I could have told him that swimming thing in his vial wasn't what the teacher wanted. I waited for Mr. Allen to tell him to take his hell-gra-whatever back and find a real bug.

Mr. Allen handed the vial back to Nick. "A hellgrammite is the larva—or the young form—of a dobsonfly. A true insect with six legs, two antennae, and three body parts. See if you can find a picture of a mature one, Nick."

That swimming thing was an insect? I couldn't believe it. And of course it had to be something interesting. *A real beaut,* the teacher had said. I rolled my eyes.

Mr. Allen turned to me. "And what did you find, Nadie?"

I handed him my vial. "It's a pillbug," I said. It had curled into a tight, round ball.

"It's buglike," Mr. Allen said, giving it back to me, "but it's not an insect."

"Not an insect?" I repeated. My face got hot.

"When is a bug not a bug?" Max asked, pretending to be all interested.

"That's the mystery Nadie will solve for us today," Mr. Allen said, smiling my way.

Right. Like I was interested in solving mysteries for Mr. Allen. I clamped my mouth shut and stared long and hard at a blue pushpin on the bulletin board. *Pillbug has the word bug right in it,* I thought. I didn't care what Mr. Allen said about it, it had to be a bug.

"How about you, Summer?" Mr. Allen asked.

"I took this off of my dog Toby," she said, handing him her vial.

Mr. Allen held it up so we could all see.

I couldn't help it. I had to look.

"Ah, a tick," our teacher said. "Since insects have six legs, this must be another non-insect mystery."

I counted its eight tiny brown legs wriggling as the bloated tick tried to right itself. It looked like it still had a piece of Toby's skin in its pincer mouth.

Summer took her vial back and waved it around for everyone to admire. She hadn't done the homework right, either, but she didn't seem to care at all that her tick wasn't really an insect. "It sucked Toby's blood," she said. "That's why it's so fat."

"Gross!" said Max.

"Eew!" Lacey screwed her eyes shut.

Why is she pretending ticks are so terrible? I thought. I knew for a fact that Lacey had pulled lots of ticks off her terrier, Digger, just last summer.

"Just wait 'til you see mine!" Owen chortled. He whisked his vial out of the desk with a flourish. Yellowy white worms writhed in a putrid-looking mass.

"Hah-hah!" he shouted. "Maggots!"

"Another example of larvae—this type is probably the young form of a house fly," Mr. Allen said. "Let's move on to Group One." He walked across the classroom.

"Blech." Jess made a face.

"Personally, I think Summer's is grosser," Max observed.

"Yeah, me too," Lacey agreed.

Owen slammed his vial down. "Maggots are grossest," he insisted. He scowled at Summer.

"Maybe," said Summer, "but can maggots dig into your skin and suck your blood?"

"Who thinks the tick wins?" Max said.

Everyone in our group raised their hands.

Summer turned a satisfied smile on Owen.

The moment I saw the look on Summer's face, I knew for sure that she couldn't care less if her tick was an insect or a reptile or a bird, as long as it was better than Owen's maggots. "Better" meaning "worse," of course. I figured now was a good time to go back to my policy of staying away from both of them.

When each group had finished showing their finds, Mr. Allen asked all of us to go back to our seats. "Each of our specimens has its own charms," he said. "Now let's take a closer look using the microscopes. Be sure you can identify your classroom visitor, then get to know those your classmates have collected as well."

"But what if you brought in something that's not an insect, like my tick?" Summer waved her vial around.

"Learning how non-insect arthropods are similar to and different from insects is an important part of our study," the teacher said. "I'd like all of you to keep your observations and drawings in your science lab notebook, and don't forget to pick up your homework packet. After lunch we'll put together our bug habitats."

I had to admit I was surprised when I finally figured out that my pillbug was a crustacean, which meant it was more closely related to marine creatures like lobsters and crayfish than bugs. It used its chewing, scraping mouthparts to eat bits of plants that rotted on the ground. *That's good,* I thought. *It can probably eat a potato, too.* Under the microscope I saw that it was covered with shiny sections, one overlapping the other, and had dainty legs that moved in waves. I made a sketch of it in my notebook.

Gordon had what I thought was the best find—a small dragonfly with a bent, blue body.

"Can I draw yours?" I asked him.

Gordon tilted his head up and down, up and down. "Affirma-tive," he said in his mechanical monotone. He swiveled his head and body away in one motion and lowered his pencil to his lab notebook. I took my time drawing the delicate net pattern of the dragonfly's wing veins. After a while, Gordon turned back to me on his robot axis. He bent forward and tipped his head down to examine my drawing.

"Accu-rate re-pre-sen-ta-tion," he said. He pushed his notebook toward me. He'd done his drawing while looking at the dragonfly under the microscope. It was beautiful.

"Wow," I said, impressed.

He ducked his head. His dark hair stood up in a shiny cowlick, and his scalp flushed a little pinkish. I picked up my lab notebook and moved on to sketch other people's bugs. I skipped the tick and the maggots.

* * *

Mr. Allen let me stay in the classroom at lunchtime to finish my sketches. I didn't get much drawing done, though, because I was too busy eavesdropping on the *Spark*'s editorial meeting. I couldn't believe how many submissions Gordon and Jess wanted to choose for this week's issue. And lots of them weren't even about bugs. How could Mr. Allen let them wreck the magazine like that? *He just has to let me work on it,* I thought. *I'd do such a great issue. And I'd never let trouble find its way anywhere near the* Spark *again.*

"Nadie, ah, don't you need to be somewhere?" Mr. Allen's voice shook me out of my thoughts.

"Yeah," I said, remembering that trouble seemed to have a

way of finding me lately. Reluctantly I put away my notebook and left for my cleanup punishment at the zoofeteria.

The tables were empty and all of the kids were lined up to leave. Mrs. Wolfowitz was standing guard at the far end of the room. I sidled in and stood with my back against the broom closet as the throng of kids crushed by.

I saw Nick's face in the crowd, but he didn't see me. He had this dull look about him, like he didn't care what direction he got pushed in or what he was doing. I couldn't stand to see him looking like that.

Without thinking, I stuck my hand out and grabbed his arm. "Nick."

"Together again!" someone sang out. I dropped Nick's arm and looked around. The fifth grader from the media center was pointing at us. "These two like each other," he crowed.

I heard shouts of "Oooh!" and "Let's see!" from a knot of boys nearby. One of them shoved Nick into me. "Go on," another kid called out, making loud kissing noises. "Go for it!"

They were all laughing at us. The space around me was collapsing, and I couldn't breathe. Nick struggled to get away. His ears were such a dark purple I couldn't see any freckles at all.

"Get off!" He squirmed free of their pushing hands without even a glance at me. "I don't like her!" he shouted at the crowd. "We're not even friends!" He broke through the group of boys, elbowing past anyone who got in his way. I was left standing alone in the middle of the circle. My face was burning.

"Guess you lost your boyfriend," the fifth grader from the media center jeered. "Too bad for you." He and his friends jostled each other through the doorway. Then the lunchroom was empty.

There is no such thing as a boy who's a friend, I thought. I yanked open the closet door and hauled out the bucket and the mop.

* * *

When I got back to class after mopping the cafeteria floor, I noticed a bad smell hanging on the air. *The telltale stink of a rat,* I thought, glowering sideways at Nick. I turned my back on him. As far as I was concerned, Nick Fanelli didn't exist.

Mr. Allen had cut all of the soda bottles in half, even the extra ones Lacey had brought. They were lined up on the counter, waiting to be used for our bug habitats. I put pebbles and dirt in the bottom of one of the extras and added a cotton ball soaked with water. The odor in the room got stronger. Other kids were noticing it, too.

"What's that smell?" asked Alima, wrinkling her nose.

"Eeew," said Lacey. "Open a window!"

"Owen," Mr. Allen said. "What exactly did you bring in to feed your maggots?"

"I found them in the top of our compost pile," Owen said, "so I brought some compost."

"I think you're going to have to dispose of it," Mr. Allen told him.

Owen went to the coatroom and came back with a plastic bag full of greenish black slime. "Look," he said, waving it toward Summer. "Your dinner."

Here we go again, I thought. I shifted my chair back away from the desks.

"I didn't have to bring anything to feed my tick," Summer said. "He already ate Toby's blood." She grinned.

"That's it, Mr. Allen," Lacey groaned. "I want to change groups!"

"Owen, take that bag to the Dumpster immediately," Mr. Allen said.

Owen held the bag up to his nose, and then offered it to Mr. Allen. "This doesn't stink that bad," Owen announced, sounding disappointed.

Mr. Allen took a careful sniff of Owen's maggot food. "Not particularly inviting, but you're right, it is not the source of our problem."

The smell was making me want to stop breathing. Mr. Allen tried opening a window, but the wind sent the papers on his desk sailing around the room. He opened the door to the hall.

"I'll see if the janitor can come help us," he said.

I finished my habitat and put my pillbug in. I covered the open end with a piece of netting held on by a rubber band.

"That's nice," Summer said, peering into my habitat.

"I'm going to get its food," I said. I went to the coatroom for my potato bag. When I unzipped my backpack and pulled out the bag, the stench almost knocked me flat. It was worse than Mom's burned soufflé. It was worse than week-old thermos milk. It was even worse than the dead possum Nick and I found in the woods last year. I pinched my nose and held the bag at arm's length. A dark liquid oozed from the bottom.

"Look out!" I cried, sprinting across the room toward the trash can.

"Aughhh!" Jess yelled as I went by. Some kids held their noses and others pulled the necks of their shirts up over their faces. Everyone was groaning. Lacey and Alima ran out of the room.

Owen stepped in my path. "My maggots will eat that!" he said, swiping the bag from my hand. "Or,"—he turned and dangled it toward Summer—"maybe your tick wants some?"

Summer made her thumb and finger into pincers. "Ticks drink blood, remember?" She snapped her pincers at Owen.

"Summer, don't," I cried.

"Get your claws away!" Owen yelled. He swung the bag back.

It came toward me. I grabbed for it but missed. The bag caught me square on the shoulder and burst open. Stinking, rotted, liquid potato soaked through my clothes and oozed down my front in a slimy drizzle. Mr. Allen and the janitor arrived in the doorway as I started to gag. In a blur Mr. Allen ripped the curtain from the coatroom doorway, wrapped me up in it, and swept me out into the hallway. Holding his breath, he ran with me down the hall.

* * *

I had to shower in the nurse's office. I ran the water as hot as it would go and filled the room with steam. While I was in the shower the nurse knocked, then came in to seal my clothes in a plastic garbage bag.

"How are we doing, dear?" she called through the curtain.

I shrank against the far wall. *Leave me alone,* I thought. *I'm never coming out of here.*

"I brought you some clothes," she said. "I'll just leave them here on the chair."

Everyone knew about the clothes in the nurse's office. She'd told us about them right after she'd showed us the mortifying movie called *Your Changing Body*. If any of us ever *needed* to have a shower, she'd explained, we could come to her office and she'd give us those nice, clean fifty-year-old clothes from the lost and found. It was a joke throughout the whole school. Only now I wasn't laughing.

I scrubbed my skin until it felt raw, then scrubbed some more. I rinsed my mouth and spit. I even snorted water out of my nose. I knew I'd never stop smelling those rotten potatoes as long as I lived. And there was no way I was putting on those castoff clothes and going back to class.

"Dear," the nurse called in again. "I told Mr. Allen that you'd be fine and that the school day is almost over, but he seemed to think that you ought to go home now. Your father is on the way to pick you up. Turn off the water and get dressed."

I waited until I heard her close the door, and then I shut off the water. If all I had to do was put on those clothes and run to Dad's car, I could probably manage it. On the chair I found new underwear, still in the package. That was a relief. The corduroy pants were so long I tripped over the legs and had to hold the waist up around my middle in a bunch.

"Nadie?" It was Dad's voice.

I yanked the shirt over my head. It felt worn out, but it had a familiar, comforting sort of smell.

Dad was holding the garbage bag full of my putrid clothes when I came out of the shower room. "Ready to go?" he asked.

I nodded. We hurried out and got in the car. Raindrops splattered the windshield. I closed my eyes and rested my cheek on the shirt's soft sleeve. I listened to the soothing *swish-click, swish-click* of the windshield wipers as Dad pulled out of the school parking lot.

"That was nice of Nick to lend you his favorite shirt," Dad said. "I thought he'd lost it."

I opened my eyes and looked down. I was wearing Nick's blue and gray striped shirt.

I started to cry.

11
THE WAY THINGS SEEM

My tears dripped onto Nick's shirt and soaked together in a big damp patch. Dad reached over and took my hand. He kept driving. When my last sob had wrung itself out, I watched the sheets of rain pounding against my side window.

Dad squeezed my hand and let it go. "I think we'll just toss the whole bag of clothes right in the trash can when we get home. What do you say?"

"Nick isn't my friend anymore," I whispered. The car rolled through the gray-black streets, and we took a right onto Laurel Road.

"You and Nick have had disagreements before," Dad said. "You always work it out."

I shook my head.

"I think it'll be okay. You and Nick are buddy-pals." He drove up Bayberry, then we turned onto our street.

My chest felt achy and hollow. "Boys and girls can't be friends." I choked out the words.

"Whoa," Dad said. He tapped the steering wheel with his fingers.

"It's the way things are," I told him, "when you get older."

"Maybe that's not the way things really are," Dad said after a minute. "Maybe that's just the way things seem right now." He pulled into our driveway. Out my window I saw a chalky, wet blur where Brambletown used to be.

The way things seem is the way they are, I thought.

* * *

I lay on my bed and listened to rain drumming on the roof. I'd already counted seventy-three dime-sized smudges on the ceiling, and I was only halfway across. Nick and I had made the smudges by bouncing a racquetball in my room on lots of other rainy days. Rainy day racquetball was just another thing I could add to my list of "no mores"—no more Brambletown, no more *Springville Spark*, no more expeditions to the stream. No more best friend.

I rolled off the bed and went to sit at my desk. From my window, Nick's house looked dark and empty, but I knew it wasn't. He had to be home from school by now, since Dad had left five minutes ago to pick up Zack. I turned my back to the window. Why should I care about Nick anyway?

I pulled the lab packet Mr. Allen had given us for homework out of my backpack and tossed it onto the desk. It landed with a this-will-take-forever kind of *thunk*. I flipped through the pages. There was a lot of information about all of the biggest insect groups, like beetles, butterflies, and bees. Mr. Allen had left a big space at the end of each section for notes or drawings or whatever we wanted to add about the insects in that group.

I decided to cut out the bug sketches I'd made in my lab notebook and glue them into the empty spaces. I hunted in my desk for scissors. They weren't in the top drawer, and they weren't in any of the side drawers. They weren't on my dresser, under the bed, or on the windowsill. They weren't in the closet.

I searched through my desk again. "Why can't anything be where it's supposed to be?" I yelled, slamming the top drawer shut. A pile of old *Spark* issues started spilling off the desktop one by one. I shoved the whole stack over onto the floor.

Zack stuck his head in the door. He marched over and grabbed one of the class magazines. "I like this one!" The cover was a picture of a train I'd drawn, using his engine as a model. It ripped off in his hands.

"Give me that!" I snatched the paper from him.

Zack's chin started to wobble. "But I like it," he said. His eyes filled with tears.

Great job, I thought. *Sister of the Year.* The missing scissors, the rotten potatoes, Nick's outburst—none of it had anything to do with my almost-three-year-old brother and I knew it.

"I'm sorry, Zacky," I said. I scooped him onto my bed. "If you like that picture, you can have it. I'll even hang it on the wall in your room. Want me to?" I smoothed the magazine cover out on the desk.

Zack nodded. "Next to my bed." He snuffled and rubbed his eyes with his fists.

I buried my nose in his neck and breathed in his warm, muffiny smell. He wiggled out of my hug.

* * *

After we hung his picture, I got the folding table from the closet and we made a tent with his blanket. He dragged in a box of plastic animals and set them up in rows.

"I'm the teacher," he said.

"Again?" I joked.

"Hey in there," Dad called. "You guys ready for a snack?"

"No!" Zack protested. "Tigers and dinosaurs are doing school."

"How about if I play school with you and the tigers so Nadie can get on with her homework?"

"Okay," Zack said.

Dad pushed his way into the tent and sat all over Zack and me.

"Dad, get off!" I said, laughing. Zack giggled. I crawled out. I realized that I still hadn't found the scissors for my lab project.

I knocked on the tabletop. "Dad? Do you know where any scissors are?"

"I think there are some down on my desk," Dad said.

I went downstairs to his office. The computer was on, and I signed on to the Internet out of habit. While it was connecting, I hunted around for the scissors. I looked through the desk drawers and on Dad's drafting table. I finally found them under a pile of envelopes. I glanced at the computer screen. On my buddy list, Engineermom was highlighted, and there was an instant message.

Hi, sweetie! Are you there?

I sighed, feeling worn out flat. Mom would want to help, but I just couldn't wring myself through everything that had happened again. I knew Dad would fill her in when she got home, their hushed voices weaving through my dreams in the middle of the night.

Just then brackets appeared around the screen name Engineermom. She had signed off. I stared at my empty buddy list, then signed off and picked up the scissors.

It seemed kind of old-fashioned to be cutting and pasting with my hands instead of cutting and pasting on the computer. But scanning my sketches and all those lab packet pages would be more work than it was worth. Anyway, it would be fun to use my colored pencils instead of my painting program to fill in the sketches.

My good art pencils—the ones you could dip in water and use like paints—were up in my room. I dropped my packet and the scissors on the kitchen table on my way upstairs. Muffled music from Zack's tape player drifted out from under his closed door. Zack was singing along with his favorite tape, *Sing Along with Bill*. I didn't hear Dad's off-key voice, so I had a pretty good idea that Dad was snoozing instead of singing along with Bill.

Back in the kitchen, I filled a cup with water to use with the colored pencils. Outside the window the gloomy day was turning into a murky night. As I looked at the light coming from the house across the street, the gray shape of a person passed in front of it—a person with a shopping bag. I set the water in the sink, slipped into the pantry, and closed the door most of the way, crouching behind it. Two seconds later I heard a knock. The kitchen door opened.

"Hallo?" Mrs. Fanelli called.

I tried to make myself into a small, tight ball like my pillbug.

"I have the dinner," Mrs. Fanelli called. Her footsteps creaked across the kitchen floor. She stopped at the door to the pantry.

"Hmmm," she said loudly. "No one here."

I heard her open the refrigerator. Its motor started to whir.

"If someone was here, I'd tell them something."

I had to move, ever so carefully, and stick my ear near the edge of the door so I could hear over the humming refrigerator.

"If someone was here," she said, "I'd tell them what a sad boy I have in my house."

I shrank back into the dark of the pantry. Mrs. Fanelli slammed the refrigerator door.

"I don't want to have this sad boy. If someone was here, I'd say you come right now and fix him." Mrs. Fanelli's footsteps creaked across the floor again, and the kitchen door opened. "I can't fix him," she said, more quietly. The door closed behind her.

Still crouching in the pantry, I hugged my knees and rocked, my cheek resting on the soft sleeve of Nick's shirt. Part of me wanted to run after Mrs. Fanelli and wrap my arms around her. But I didn't know how to fix anything, so I stayed put.

12

ANOTHER POTATO

The next day I slipped into my seat and glanced around uneasily. Most kids were near the window checking on their bug habitats.

"Eew!" Lacey wailed.

Thinking she'd found a blob of my rotten potato from yesterday, I scrunched down.

"My moth laid eggs!" she said.

"Cool!" Max said. "Let's see."

Kids crowded to look at Lacey's moth eggs. I didn't see Nick over there. Mr. Allen was crouching next to the bookcase. *He's probably still cleaning from yesterday,* I thought. The air stung my eyes and nose. Ammonia with an underwhiff of rotten potato. I wanted to turn right around and go home. I opened my desk and stuck my head inside. Maybe I could just stay that way for the rest of the year.

Next to me, Lacey's desk lid swung up just a little. I saw a hand slip a red pouch into her desk, and I peered around the edge of mine. Max was walking away. *What did he hide in there?* I wondered. I hoped he wasn't getting in on the gross-out contest. If he put something disgusting in Lacey's desk, we'd all hear about it. And because I sat next to her, I'd hear about it extra loud.

I heard Nick plunk into his seat across from me and I forgot about Lacey's desk. On my way to school, with a warm breeze turning the corner on spring, I'd tried look at the good side of things. At school I didn't have to pretend anymore that Nick wasn't my friend. He wasn't. I had almost convinced myself it would be a big relief. It wasn't.

Summer scraped her chair closer to mine. I moved farther under my desk lid, shuffling books like I was looking for something. I had to stay away from her. Owen may have been the one swinging the potato bag, but Summer had kept egging him on. I was through being dragged into their gross-out war.

My desk lid swung up a bit. Summer crowded her head and shoulders in underneath with me. I moved as far to the other side as I could.

"Don't worry, it's over," she said. My desktop rested on her head. "I told Owen I'm not going to try and outdo him anymore. I told him I give in. I told him he's the King of Disgusting."

I wasn't sure if I'd heard her right. Summer had backed down? I was having trouble picturing it.

"That's what I did." Summer nodded. The desk lid bobbed up and down. "I told Owen he won."

Yeah, until the next time I'm standing between you and a bag of slime, I thought. *Then the game will be right back on. No thanks.* I raised the lid and sat up straight in my seat. Summer scooted her chair back over to her desk.

After a minute, I noticed something. Instead of the faint but still-awful stench of ammonia and rotten potato, the classroom was starting to smell like Sunday mornings. Mr. Allen hadn't been cleaning under the bookcase. He'd plugged in a coffeemaker. I closed my eyes and let the delicious coffee aroma carry me home to our happy, sunny kitchen. Maybe Dad was right—maybe things weren't as bad as they seemed.

"Hazelnut," I said to nobody in particular. I opened my eyes. That's when I saw the potato sitting on the corner of my desk. I felt all of the air go out of me like a dead balloon.

I swept the potato into my desk, hoping no one else had seen it. A tiny piece of paper fluttered to the floor. I felt Nick looking at me, and I flicked an angry glance his way. His face was all red and he jumped right up and hurried to the coatroom. Had Nick left the potato on my desk to remind me of what happened yesterday? Could he really be mean enough to want to rub it in?

Summer leaned way over in her chair, practically doing a handstand to get the piece of paper. She handed it to me. "Did this come with the—?"

"Yes," I cut her off. I didn't want her to say "potato" out loud. I didn't really want to read the note, either, but I had to know who had left the potato on my desk. "This is for your pillbug," the note read. It was printed on computer paper and could have been from anybody.

I caught my breath. What did this mean? Was it a terrible joke, or was someone trying to help? I'd been full to the brim with my own misery and had forgotten all about feeding my poor pillbug. With that hazelnut coffee scent wafting through the air around me, I decided to believe someone was trying to help. I opened my desk and took out the potato. At the sink, I washed it and cut off two small pieces.

The bell rang and Mrs. Novotny came into the room. The kids from her class were lined up outside in the hall with their coats on, ready to go out for gym. "You have the best-smelling room in the building, Mr. Allen," she said.

"Why, thank you, Mrs. Novotny," Mr. Allen said with a smile. "May I offer you a cup of coffee?"

"I was hoping you'd say that. I'll enjoy it during my planning period." Mrs. Novotny held up a purple and white mug. Mr. Allen poured.

I dropped the bits of potato into my bug habitat. The pillbug seemed okay. I wondered if it was going to eat the potato. I wondered if Summer could really stop competing with Owen.

Mostly I wondered if Nick Fanelli was back to just pretending he wasn't my friend.

13

SUMMER'S KIND OF FUN

I went through the hot lunch line to buy milk. The sludgy smell of chop suey hung over everything like a fog. Lacey pushed her lunch tray along ahead of me to the cash register. She paid the lunch lady with money from a red pouch.

"Hey, Lacey, that's your lunch money?" I asked. "What was Max doing with it? I saw him put it inside your desk this morning."

"No he didn't," Lacey said quickly.

"But I—"

"He didn't!" Lacy insisted. She hurried off to sit with Jess and Alima.

I didn't know why she was acting so weird, and I didn't much care. I sat at a table by myself to think. I missed the quiet of our lunchtime meetings, and I missed working on the *Spark*. But at least I was done with the awful job of cleaning up the lunch mess for Mrs. Wolfowitz. She was in her chair at the center of the room with her eyes closed, and I hoped as hard as I could that she'd stay that way.

I took a container of fruit salad, celery with peanut butter, sesame crackers, and a juice box out of my lunch bag. Summer parked herself on the bench next to me.

"Hi," she said.

I ducked my head and started eating my fruit salad, but it was hard to completely ignore someone who kept acting that friendly.

"What took me so long," she said, as if I'd been wondering, "was I dropped my milk money and it rolled under the steam tables and everywhere. It was all pennies, too!" She laughed.

I couldn't help it. The picture of Summer grabbing for pennies under the lunch ladies' feet made me smile a little. And the odd thing about smiling is how it makes you feel sort of relaxed and nice, even when you're trying not to be. I watched Summer dig around in her plastic bag. She pulled out a paper cup with another cup upside down over the top of it.

"I was in kind of a rush this morning when I grabbed this chili," she said. "I probably should have gone with the thermos."

"Um-hmm," I said, swallowing a bite of celery. Sauce had leaked out of the bottom cup, staining it greasy orange. The thought of cold, lumpy meat and sticky beans made my stomach flip.

"My mom's chili is really great when it's hot," Summer said, as if she was trying to convince herself. She spooned in a mouthful and started chewing. I went back to my lunch, hoping to get through the period without any new catastrophes. While I was eating, I heard a really loud growl coming from the direction of Summer's stomach. After a couple of minutes, I stole a sideways look at her. She wasn't chewing anymore.

The stained paper cup was sitting on the table in front of her. Even the best chili in the world couldn't taste all that great when it was cold. I could see that there was nothing else in her plastic bag. My bag, on the other hand, still had some celery with peanut butter and a few more crackers. Her stomach rumbled again.

I held out the celery. "I'm full. You want this?"

She unwrapped a stalk, turned it over a couple of times, and bit into it. "Kind of weird, but pretty good," she decided.

I didn't see how celery with peanut butter was any weirder than the stuff Summer brought, but I didn't say anything. I gave her half of the crackers, and we had just finished the last of my lunch when the bell rang for recess.

On our way out I tossed my bag into the trash, then stopped. "Ugh! I forgot about my fruit salad bowl." I peered at the gray chop suey sauce and limp bean sprouts oozing down the sides of the garbage can.

Without hesitating even a second, Summer reached in and rescued my lunch bag. She picked out the plastic container and held it out to me, letting the paper bag fall back in the can.

"Even *I* don't dive into the lunchroom garbage," Owen chortled as he walked out the door. The two boys right behind him laughed, too.

Summer acted like nothing had happened. "You can have my bag to put it in if you want," she said to me.

I didn't have a better idea, so I said, "Thanks."

I took the bag, and she dropped my container inside, smiling that wide-open smile of hers. Staying mad at Summer took a lot of work. I left the bag near the door and let the warm hallway sunshine sweep us outside and up the hill to the edge of the field.

Summer flopped on the grass, even though it was damp. She picked up an acorn cap and put it on her pointer finger. Then she put a second acorn cap on the other pointer. "Hello." She made one finger nod to the other. "Hello."

I laughed, then caught myself. Most of our classmates would make fun of playing with acorns like little kids. *They'd probably make fun of Brambletown, too,* I thought. But Summer didn't care about what other kids said or did, as long as *she* was having fun. I thought about Nick being my friend and then not being my friend, and how everything had changed when we moved up into fourth grade. That definitely wasn't fun. Then I remembered that Summer's kind of fun also included pushing Owen until he went too far. It was all too confusing.

Summer crouched at the edge of the trees and moved some wet leaves around with her other hand, making a square. "This is a house for my acornheads," she said. She marched her fingers through an imaginary doorway.

For right now, I decided not to care about anything. I helped Summer pile the brown leaves into different shapes, like lots of little houses. The sun warmed my back. "You should have seen the town we made in our cul-de-sac," I said.

"I could come see it after school."

I thought about the chalky blur that had once been Brambletown. "You could have, but it's not—"

A shadow moved across our leaf piles. I stood up in a hurry. Gordon was standing there, shifting from one foot to the other.

"Mister-Allen-sent-me," he said in his robot voice. "You-are-needed-for-the-*Spark*-layout." He turned and marched stiffly toward the school building.

This was great news. They couldn't even do one issue without me. Maybe Mr. Allen had really meant to replace me just for Monday and Tuesday—the days I'd owed Mrs. Wolfowitz. Would Nick be back, too? I wondered. I filled my chest with a big gulp of the damp, mossy air. The warm spring day made me believe good things were just waiting to happen.

"See you," Summer said. She was pushing at a pile of leaves, her wheat-blonde hair hanging in front of her face. She tucked it behind her ears. Her fingers left a line of dirt on her forehead. She looked up and smiled. I smiled, too. Then I ran down the hill and followed Gordon back to class.

* * *

When I got to the classroom, Gordon and Jess were sitting with Mr. Allen at a computer. Nick wasn't there. *Maybe he's on his way,* I thought.

"Hello, Nadie," Mr. Allen said. "I hoped that as the former art editor of the *Spark* you would be willing to share your layout expertise with the new editors." He got up from his chair and motioned for me to sit down.

Gordon stared straight ahead at the computer screen. Jess was reading a submission.

"You mean you want me to show Gordon how I decide where to put the artwork?" I asked. I picked up one of the drawings on the desk and looked it over. "Well, first I—"

Mr. Allen didn't wait for me to finish. "Why don't you start by demonstrating to Gordon and Jess how to insert pictures into the publishing document?"

I slumped in my chair. *So that's it,* I thought. *I'm only here because Mr. Allen doesn't know the first thing about computers.* I wasn't back on the *Spark* at all. I pushed the mouse around and around on its pad.

"Nadie?" Mr. Allen said.

I made the arrow point at the little picture of an open newspaper on the desktop. "This is the Publish It Now program icon," I droned, sounding a little like Gordon.

I went through the steps one at a time. I showed them how to start the program, scan pictures, and import text files. Mr. Allen jotted down lots of notes, but anyone could see he wasn't getting it. After a while he stopped jotting. Then he went to his desk and graded papers. Gordon and Jess figured out how to work the program right away. Especially Gordon. When I showed him how I used different kinds of artwork in the layout, he got as excited as a robot boy could get, and he immediately started trying some new layout tricks of his own.

Nick was first in from recess, so he saw me there still working with Gordon and Jess. He tried to act like he didn't care, but I could tell he did. I knew that Nick blamed me for getting us kicked off the magazine. Now it probably seemed to him like I was back on the *Spark* and he was left out. Of course none of that was true. *He shouldn't always be blaming me for everything,* I thought, glowering inside. Other kids piled through the door.

"You guys can take it from here," I told Gordon and Jess.

Summer came in holding up one hand with acorn-capped fingers and carrying the plastic bag in the other. "You left this in the hall. Want me to put it in your cubby?"

"I'll take it," I muttered. I was still seething about Nick and the *Spark.*

"Hey, Nadie!" Owen shouted from the doorway. "That's not yours." He dashed over and grabbed the bag from me. "It's hers." He swung the bag toward Summer.

"It's her bag, but it's *my* fruit salad container." I said each word slowly to make sure Owen understood. The last thing I needed was some stupid trouble from him. I reached for the bag.

Owen jerked it away and the container fell out on the floor. The lid flew off. Inside was something mud-colored and dry. It was flat, like it had been run over by a steamroller. It had four legs splayed out at weird angles. A really long time ago it might have been a frog.

"What do you say to that?" Owen shouted at Summer. He was practically jumping up and down.

I looked at Summer and stepped back.

"You did it again." She nodded to Owen. "Yup," she said, pointing at the frog with one acorn-capped finger, "that's definitely the grossest thing I've ever seen."

Owen stared at Summer. He picked up the frog and started to wave it toward her, but then he stopped and pulled it back. His face turned red. "Okay then," he mumbled. He spun away and went to his seat. I'd never seen him stop in the middle of one of his crazy plans like that before, so it was really something.

The frog-in-the-box could have turned into a revolting disaster, but it hadn't, even though that kind of disaster would have been Summer's kind of fun. She'd kept her word to me about not starting up with Owen anymore, and that was really something, too.

14

A Kid I Used To Play With

Sparrows jumped in and out of starry forsythia tangles at the edge of the sidewalk. Purple crocuses poked out of the dark earth next to mailboxes all along the way home from school. The whole world was wide awake for spring. When I neared the corner of Broom and Laurel, I closed my eyes and tipped my face to the sun. I guess part of me hoped to find Nick, but he wasn't there. It felt long, walking home alone from the empty corner for the third day in a row.

As I headed up our driveway, I heard Dad's favorite oldies station blasting through the open window. The kitchen smelled like warm, gooey chocolate. A red plastic kayak just big enough for Zack sat on the kitchen table.

"Colorful snack," I yelled over the music to Dad. "Got any paddles to go with that?"

Dad turned down the radio. "Everybody's a comedian," he said. He glanced behind me. I knew he was looking for Nick, but he recovered quickly. "Keep up those oh-so-funny jokes and you just might miss the real snack." He leaned against the counter and crossed his arms.

"What real snack?" I tried to dodge around him, but he kept stepping in my way and holding out his arms to fend me off. I ducked under one arm, and he caught me in a headlock. I found myself face to face with a plate of his chocolate fudge. "Dad, you're the best!" I put my arms around his waist and squeezed.

"I don't know what got into me," he laughed. "Must be the weather."

Somebody knocked on the door. Had Nick smelled the fudge from across the street?

"Well, hello there," Dad said. He pushed open the screen door.

It wasn't Nick. I was half disappointed and half mystified when Summer walked in and stood in the middle of our kitchen. Her shoulders were scrunched up near her ears. She took in everything without moving her head. She looked the way I felt when I met all of her cats.

"You can come in, too," Dad said. He was still holding the door open. The fat orange cat skittered past him and twined through Summer's legs. I was glad to see Contact. I squatted next to Summer and scratched the cat between her silky ears. She purred.

"Dad, this is Summer," I said. "Summer Crawford. She's new in my class at school. And this"—I pointed to the cat—"is Contact."

"Nice to meet you," Dad said. "And you, too, Contact." The big cat stretched and yawned like she'd been in our kitchen all of her life. Dad ran his hand along her back. "Well, I'd better go pick up Zack," he said. "See you guys in a bit."

Summer watched our car back down the driveway. She let out her held-in breath. "Who's Zack?" she asked.

"My little brother," I said, getting the plate of fudge. "He's almost three."

Summer eyed the plate suspiciously. "I thought your dad was some kind of health food nut," she said. "So what's that made out of, anyway?"

I grinned and handed her a piece. "Don't ask, just eat," I said. "Trust me."

Summer took a piece and touched it with her tongue. Then she popped the whole thing in her mouth and chewed with her eyes closed. Contact leaped onto a chair and put her paws on the table. She leaned over and tested the red kayak in a few places with her nose. Then she climbed inside.

"Is this your brother's?" Summer asked, pointing at the kayak.

"It's probably a prop," I told her. "My dad's been shooting some photo layouts for *Outdoor Fun* magazine."

"Your dad's a photographer? Cool! Can I see some of his pictures?"

I took Summer on a photo tour. She laughed at the pictures of Mom's soufflé disaster on the kitchen bulletin board. When she saw the framed picture of me holding Zack, she put her hand out as if to touch the tiny bundle in the picture that was my newborn brother. We moved on, and Contact padded after us into the living room. Summer stopped in front of a picture of my uncle standing in his apartment hallway. Francis the Evil peered around an open door in the background.

"Was this for a magazine, or do you actually know that cat?" Summer asked.

I looked at Francis, his eyes glowing in the photo like two pale lamps. "That's Francis," I said with a sigh. "He's my uncle's cat."

"I'd watch out for Francis," Summer said. "That cat's up to no good. There's something about him—the look in those eyes." She shook her head in disgust. "He could give cats a bad reputation."

"Uh-huh," I said.

"I'm not kidding, Nadie."

"Oh, believe me, I know," I assured her.

"Who are these of?" Summer asked, moving to the opposite side of the room. She stood in front of an entire wall covered with black-and-white photos of me when I was really little. I thought maybe she didn't recognize me since my hair used to be a lot lighter, and curly like Mom's. There was a picture of me in a plastic swimming pool, me on the swings, me up to my elbows in finger paints, me eating my first birthday cake. And with me in every single photo—in the pool, on the swings, and covered with paint and cake—was my best friend, Nick.

"Who's this?" Summer asked again.

"Me," I said.

"And your buddy?" Summer prompted.

I stared at the picture of us on the swings. I could never be sure if it was a real memory or a memory I'd made from stories, but I knew the moment by heart. Nick and I were three, and we were singing. Even in the photo's gray tones the sun gleamed on his red-gold hair.

"That's a kid I used to play with," I told her.

Summer looked at those photos for a long time. "Your dad's a pretty good photographer," she said.

* * *

"Kitty!" my brother shouted. He ran across the room, heading for Contact.

"Zack!" I warned. "Be careful!"

"Don't worry." Summer smiled. She sat down and pulled her cat closer. "This is Contact, not Francis, remember?"

The big orange cat lay down on her side. Zack put his hand on her head.

"She doesn't run away, Nadie," Zack said.

He was right. Contact didn't move. Zack put his head down on the floor and stared into the cat's green eyes. "Good kitty," he said, stroking her fur. Contact put a soft paw on his shoulder.

Dad snapped a picture from the doorway. "That's a keeper," he said. "Hey, Zack? I've got to shoot some pictures of this kayak. Want to take a walk to the stream?"

"With the kitty?" Zack asked. He snuggled closer to Contact.

"I don't know," Dad said. "What do you say, Summer? Would you and Contact like to come with us?"

Summer nodded her head, a blush spreading across her pale skin. It dawned on me that Summer wasn't used to being around my dad. Or any dad, maybe. Dad slung the strap of his tripod over his shoulder, then handed Summer a small bag full of lenses and supplies. "Oops—forgot one thing. Be right back," he said. He pounded down the stairs to his studio.

We walked outside with Zack and Contact. Summer's bicycle was parked at the side of our driveway.

"I came over to see that skating town you made," Summer said. "Where is it?"

I couldn't help glancing over at Nick's house. I thought I saw a curtain move, but I couldn't be sure. I pointed to the cul-de-sac. "It was over there," I said. "But it washed away in the rain." I sighed. Brambletown was gone, all right.

"And we're off!" Dad came out, and the door slammed

behind him. He led the way into the woods. When we got to the spot Dad wanted to use for his photos, he gave me the job of getting Zack into the kayak. Contact was my assistant. She sat patiently with Zack until we had to put the kayak into the cold, shallow stream. Then she hopped out and stalked off into the woods nearby.

Summer was Dad's assistant. He asked her to hand him lenses and film while he worked. I noticed that at first she didn't get very close to him. After a while, though, she was checking out the camera and looking through the viewfinder. She even snapped some pictures.

Zack climbed in and out of the kayak, splashing me every time. Pretty soon we were soaked. When Dad was done, I sat my brother on a boulder to dry out. The smooth rock felt warm from the sun, and Zack tapped his red sneakers together happily. Contact leaped up next to him.

"Don't worry, Nadie," my brother told me. "Contact is not Francis."

"What does the kitty say?" I asked him.

"She says *prrrrrr.*" Zack blew air through his lips, making a slow-sounding raspberry.

I laughed. Summer was looking at us through the camera. Dad leaned in and looked over her shoulder. Contact put her front paws on Zack's legs and touched her pink nose to his. I heard the camera click.

"That's going to be the shot of the day, Summer," Dad said.

Summer pushed her hair behind her ears and grinned.

"Time to pack it in, you soggy kids," Dad told us. "Let's make sure we have everything."

"I have a hurt," Zack said proudly. He pointed to a faint red scratch on his arm.

Summer produced a plastic bandage from her pocket. "I'll fix you up, Zack," she said. He slid down off the rock and hurried over to her. Contact followed.

Dad and I carried the gear through the woods, and Summer gave Zack a piggyback ride. Contact trotted along behind us. When we reached the cul-de-sac, it wasn't empty anymore.

The streets of Brambletown had reappeared.

15

DIFFERENT SPECIES

Nick worked pretty hard out there, didn't he?" Dad was gazing out the kitchen window, a dish towel in his hand. I had just come downstairs from reading Zack his four—no, five—bedtime stories. It was only a little after seven o'clock, but it was too dark to see Brambletown anymore.

Summer had promised to come back to help work on the streets and buildings, but I wasn't sure I wanted to do it all again. It would just wash away in the next rain.

I stood next to Dad and looked out toward the dark, empty end of our street. Nick must have run outside with his chalk the minute we'd stepped into the woods. He had to have drawn like mad right up until he'd heard us tromping back. He was gone by the time we got to the street. A long sigh leaked out of me. Dad put his arm around my shoulders. I turned and buried my face in his sweater that smelled like leaves and fudge.

* * *

A little later, I went down to do some drawing on Dad's computer. I signed on to the Internet like I always did and clicked on my buddy list. Engineermom showed up. That didn't mean Mom was at her desk, but I instant-messaged her just in case.

Hi, Mom! I typed. *You there?* I hit Send. I always typed out whole words for Mom instead of using IM shorthand.

Hi, sweetie! How was your day?

Okay, I answered. *My new friend came over. Helped Dad with photo shoot in woods.*

Sounds great! Mom typed back.

I smiled. Mom was right. My day had been lots better than okay.

Another IM popped up. *Nick go too?*

I blew out a long, slow breath, then typed an answer. *No. He drew chalk roads while we were at the stream.*

I'm sure he still wants to be your friend.

I closed my eyes. I wanted to be Nick's friend, too. But things had gotten out of control. I felt the weight of those rocks coming back on my chest. *Why do kids act so stupid?* I typed.

You mean Nick?

No! My fingers flew over the keys. I knew in my heart that none of it was Nick's fault. *I mean everybody else!* My eyes stung and my throat closed up tight. It was a good thing I could bang on the keyboard and didn't have to talk. *Why can't everything just be like last year?*

Things change, I guess, Mom typed. *And hormones start to fly.*

I groaned. *Fingers in my ears!*

LOL! Mom answered.

Where'd she learn that? *Not kidding,* I typed.

OK. Just remember, Nadie… Everyone figures out this growing up thing in their own way… You will, too.

How can we figure this out if we can't even talk to each other?

I'm sure you'll find a way, Mom messaged. *Sorry, sweetie. Got to run now. Love you! Mom.*

I could see that Mom wasn't signed on anymore. *I love you, too,* I typed slowly and hit Send anyway.

NickFan wasn't showing on my buddy list. But he could have changed his screen name and I wouldn't even know about it. I clicked on the drawing program and opened a new file.

An instant message popped up from RobotGord: *Hi, it's Gordon. R U Nadie?*

Why in the world was Gordon IM-ing me? *Yes,* I typed. I hesitated, then hit Send.

Can U help with Spark *bug cover?*

Gordon had picked up on the layout program just fine in school. *U know how,* I wrote back.

I can't draw like U. Work 2 gether?

I thought about it. I guessed I could do some drawings for him the next day at lunch. He'd have to figure out how to scan the drawings into the cover, though.

OK, I typed.

I live on Laurel. B right over.

No! 2 morrow in school, I pounded at the keys. But RobotGord had already signed off.

I ran upstairs. "Dad!" I grabbed his arm. "This kid is coming over to work on a *Spark* cover with me."

Dad smiled. "Right now?" he asked. "And who might this kid be?"

"Gordon," I said, finding it hard to believe myself.

"Oh," Dad said. He looked at the clock. "Well, it is a school night, so he—Gordon is a *he*, right?"

"Yes," I said miserably.

"Well, he'll have to go home by nine, don't you think?"

I thought he should go home before he even got here, but I didn't say so. Dad went into the living room and picked up a magazine. A few minutes later Gordon knocked on the kitchen door, and I had to let him in. He went right over to the table and spread out his papers. Something about him looked different.

"Here's where I got my idea," he said. He showed me Mr. Allen's list of the different kinds of insects—the biggest insect orders—beetles, butterflies, flies, bees, and a couple of others. Then he pulled out another copy of the same list, but this one had numbers up in the tens or hundreds of thousands next to the name of each order.

"Those are the numbers of different species in each of the insect orders. I thought—well, what do you think? If we draw one bug to represent each order, but no matter what size the bug actually is, we'll make it big or small depending on how many different species of that bug there are in the world?" He looked at me eagerly.

I tried to picture it. "You mean like here where it says there are three hundred and fifty thousand kinds of beetles, we make the beetle the biggest bug in the picture? And since there are only twenty thousand different bugs in the grasshopper order, we make the grasshopper the smallest?"

"Yeah! Exactly! We could put in water, trees, and dirt, all those colors washed into the background the way you do it. See? I tried to draw the bugs." Gordon showed me a page of rough sketches. "But I'm not so good without something to draw from. I know it's a lot of drawing. We should probably put in the top seven kinds, at least, and I was hoping you might, well…" His voice trailed off.

Gordon's sketches were a decent start, but it looked like he just hadn't given each one enough time. Time was going to be a big problem if we had to finish all of these tonight.

"Wait a minute!" I exclaimed. "I've already done these!" I ran upstairs and got my science packet. I showed Gordon how I'd included a drawing for almost every major insect group. "They'll be perfect for your idea. Come on. We can use my dad's computer."

Gordon followed me downstairs. While I scanned in my bug drawings and sketched the background, he figured out how big each bug should be and where it would go. We took turns filling in extra colors. Gordon had never used a drawing stylus before.

"This works great!" he said. He added a border to the background. The cover was looking very professional.

"This was a cool idea, Gordon," I said. "Mr. Allen is really going to like it." I stepped back from the screen and squinted. My eye kept going back to one dull area on the cover. "Nope." I shook my head. "With all of the beautiful butterflies in the world, we just can't use my drawing of Lacey's boring old wheat moth."

Gordon chewed his lip. "You're right," he said. "Do you want to draw something else?" He held out the stylus.

"No," I told him. "You do." I pulled out the big butterfly guide from my dad's bookshelf and handed it to Gordon. "Pick one."

He closed his eyes and let the book fall open on its own. He started to draw with the stylus, then stopped.

"Don't worry," I said. "Just keep your eye on the picture. Start with a small shape, then add more shapes around it until you have the whole thing."

Gordon bit his lip and started drawing again. He looked back and forth from the book to the screen. I watched a series of honeycomb shapes connect into the graceful form of a swallowtail butterfly. With a few clicks, Gordon washed in a brilliant yellow.

"Wow." I nodded. "Beautiful."

He ducked his head, and I saw him smile.

"Hey!" I blurted out. "Now I know what's different about you! You're not acting like a robot!"

Gordon stood up abruptly. "Thanks for the help, Nadie," he said. "Can you print that and bring it in tomorrow?" He was already halfway up the stairs.

"Gordon, wait!" I called after him.

He stopped and turned first his head, then his arms, then his body toward me.

"Why do you do it?"

Gordon looked at the ceiling for a moment. "Robots-can-act-the-same-way-to-boy-humans-and-to-girl-humans," he said, going back to his mechanical voice. But then he added in his regular voice, "And after everyone gets used to it, no one even makes fun of them much for being robots."

I was still thinking about that long after I'd heard the screen door bang behind him.

16

THE ENORMOUSLY
BRILLIANT IDEA

When I got to school the next morning I saw Nick over by the window, pouring water into his hellgrammite habitat. He didn't look up. Why had he bothered to draw the streets for Brambletown again? I'd been chewing that around and around in my mind since breakfast. I couldn't stop thinking about it. I put my backpack in my cubby and sat down.

"Hi!" Summer said. "Guess what? My tick shriveled into a tiny raisin."

"Ugh," Lacey exclaimed loudly. She made a face and checked to see who was watching her.

A tick raisin didn't seem like a happy picture to me. "Does that mean it's—"

"Yup. Gave its life for science, I guess." Summer shook her head sadly. "I didn't feed it. I mean, whose blood was I going to give it?" She held her palms up. "Mine?"

Lacey harrumphed and swiveled around in her seat, turning her back to us.

"What are you going to do about the assignment?" I asked Summer.

"Well, there are lots more ticks where that one came from. But listen," she said, changing the subject, "I have to tell you about my great idea—"

"Nadie, would you step over here a moment, please?" Mr. Allen called from his desk. "You, too, Gordon."

Whatever idea Summer had, I wasn't going to hear about it now. I watched Gordon do his metal-boy walk to Mr. Allen's desk, then followed him. All year long I'd thought Gordon's robot act was weird and a little dumb. But now I got it. A robot could be friends with anyone—boys *and* girls—because, well, he was just a machine. I could see now that Gordon the robot was smart. Really, it was everyone else who was acting dumb.

Mr. Allen's head was bent over Gordon's *Spark* cover. "I recognize these insect sketches from your science packet, Nadie," he said without looking up. "That's a problem." He tapped the drawing and frowned.

I wasn't on the *Spark* editorial board anymore, so I probably wasn't supposed to work on the cover. What if Mr. Allen made Gordon do it all over again? Today was Thursday. He couldn't finish all those drawings in time for this issue. There'd be no *Spark* this week, and by next week we might not even be working on bugs anymore.

"But Gordon had such a great idea," I tried to explain. I saw Owen watching us and lowered my voice. "I just helped him out, that's all. It really is his work."

"No, it isn't," Mr. Allen said. He looked at me, then at Gordon. He smiled. "This work belongs to both of you. It's quite remarkable, really. You should both be extremely proud. I know that I am. This cover takes the material we've been working on and uses it in a whole new way. It also showcases each of your special talents." He looked over the drawing again and cleared his throat. "I think I feel about as happy as any teacher can feel right now," he finally said. "Thank you, Nadie." Mr. Allen shook my hand. "Thank you, Gordon." Gordon's face turned a very unrobotlike shade of red.

"But Mr. Allen, if it's good, then why is it a problem?" I asked.

"It's a problem because your name isn't on the cover along with Gordon's," Mr. Allen said, pointing to the bottom of the page. "You two had better rethink that byline. This cover shows me that we need to rethink our *Spark* editorial board as well. All students who can share ideas and work together should be able to do so—that's the whole point, after all. It's what already makes our magazine spectacular and unique." He turned toward the window. "Nick?"

Nick looked up.

"Are you free at lunchtime to go over this week's *Spark* editorial with Jess?"

Nick nodded. I saw him drum a triumphant two-fingered riff on the windowsill.

"Excellent. Yes, excellent." Mr. Allen nodded back and faced the class. "And now, entomology enthusiasts, please return to your seats and take out your insect feed journals."

* * *

We ended up having a big *Spark* organizational meeting that lasted through lunch and recess. Nearly half the class was there. Kids suggested new jobs like poetry editor, news editor, and photographer. Summer volunteered to write a pet care column. Gordon and I were in charge of cover art. Nick was back on the editorial page. Alima and Jess were going to start a new section for letters to the editor.

The busy school day went by like any other, but something had changed. Maybe it was just that heart-tingling feeling of spring breaking through, but I felt I could sense all kinds of possibilities wafting in on the breeze.

At the end of the day, Mr. Allen called me up to his desk again.

"Nadie, I was wondering something. Did you scan in all of your sketches for the cover?" he asked. "Or did you draw them with a mouse?"

"Well, I scanned in most of them," I explained. "But Gordon did the butterfly right on the computer. He didn't use a mouse, though. He used my dad's drawing stylus."

"A drawing stylus?"

I glanced at the clock, then explained how the stylus worked like a pen on a pad. "My dad's computer drawing program has lots of special tools and effects. You can do all kinds of cool things with the stylus."

"If your work is any indication, that program is a wonderful learning tool," he said. "I'd like to have something like that in our classroom. Do you know the exact name of it?"

I shifted from one foot to the other and looked at the clock again. I'd been planning to wait for Nick at the corner of Broom and Laurel after school. I was just going to come right out and ask him about Brambletown. But instead of getting to our corner first, now it looked like I wasn't going to show up at all.

"Why don't I ask my dad for more information and bring it in tomorrow?" I suggested hopefully.

"Thank you, Nadie. That would be very helpful," Mr. Allen said. "Have an imaginative afternoon!"

I raced to our corner at a flat-out run, but Nick wasn't there. I picked up a handful of pebbles from the gutter and heaved it at the stop sign. Maybe boys and girls really just couldn't be friends. I didn't know anymore.

* * *

"Hello, Your Lateness," Dad said. "Where've you been?"

"Mr. Allen kept me after class for a few minutes," I said. "He asked me for information about our computer drawing program."

"I can get that together for you." Dad jangled his car keys. "But right now I'm off to get Zack. There's pudding in the fridge." He went out. "Summer's mom phoned," he called from the driveway. "I told her your idea was okay by me and I called the town hall to get permission. Just wait for me to come back before you get started."

Town hall? I pushed open the screen door and stuck my head out. I heard the car door slam. "What idea?" I yelled. Dad waved as he drove away.

Mystified, I went to the refrigerator and took out a dish of vanilla pudding. I stared at the skin on top, examining the little lines and swirls. At first they looked like an abstract design, but after a while they started to look like a beehive and a swarm of bees. Great. Thanks to Mr. Allen, I now had insects on the brain. I stuck my spoon into the beehive first. The rest of the pudding quivered.

I took a big spoonful of beehive skin with creamy pudding underneath. The soft part melted away on my tongue, and I chewed the drier skin, then swallowed. "What idea?" I said aloud.

"My idea!" Summer opened the screen door and came in waving a can of yellow spray paint. "That's what I started to tell you this morning. I mean, why let all our work on Brambletown just wash away in the next good rain?"

I looked at the can of spray paint, then at Summer's grin. "Enormously brilliant."

"My mom gave this to me," Summer said. "It's a kind of quick-dry paint that her store's not ordering anymore."

I got another pudding out of the fridge and traded it to Summer for the spray can. While she ate, I read the back panel. At the bottom it said "Coverage: 12 square feet."

"Do you think this will be enough?" I worried. "Brambletown has lots of roads."

"Don't worry about that—come and look!" Summer pulled me outside to her bike, parked in the driveway. Contact was curled up in the kiddie trailer next to a cardboard box filled with spray cans.

"I guess old Contact's guarding the goods," Summer said, laughing.

I scratched the orange cat behind her ears. I felt the gentle, steady rhythm of her purr travel through me as I looked out at the chalk beginnings of what would be our new Brambletown.

* * *

When Dad came home, he helped us get started. The clerk at Town Hall had told him that since no houses had been built yet on the cul-de-sac it would be okay to put paint on the street surface. They'd have to repave it after houses were built anyway.

Dad showed us how to spray close to the ground and downwind so we wouldn't paint ourselves or breathe in fumes. Apparently not interested in paint, Contact stayed in the kiddie trailer. Zack bustled back and forth from the house to the driveway bringing treats and water for "kitty."

Summer and I filled in all of the chalk roads with white and pale yellow spray paint. Brambletown was taking on a bold new look. I stood up straight to stretch and admire our work.

"We have lots of other colors," Summer said, tossing through the cans in the box. "We can use them for the shops and houses. What do you want to add first?"

"A paint store," I said right away. "In honor of your mom."

Summer gave me one of her wide-open smiles. I shaded my eyes and surveyed the painted roads of Brambletown. They looked solid and permanent. I was glad Summer was here. A cloud passed over the sun, and in its shadow I had that prickly feeling of being watched. I looked over at Nick's house. His living room curtain was pulled to the side in one place. The sun came out again, flooding Brambletown with buttery light. I took a deep breath and looked back at our new roads.

"How would it be if the buildings weren't just flat—if we made them stand up somehow?" I asked Summer.

"It would be great!" she said. "We could skate or bike around them like we were in our own little town." She pursed her lips. "Do you have wood and stuff to make them with?" she asked.

"No," I told her. "I have another idea. I'll be right back."

I walked across the cul-de-sac and up Nick's driveway. My legs felt quivery like the pudding. As I raised my hand to ring the bell, the door flew open.

"Hi," Nick said.

The familiar smell of his mom's lemon furniture oil made me gulp. "Do you still have any of those plastic grocery crates?" I asked.

"You mean the ones from the store? We have lots in the garage," he said.

"I thought—I mean—I was wondering if you think they'd make good buildings for Brambletown."

"Yes, they would," he said. He rubbed the top of his head. "Do you want me to help you bring them over?"

"No," I said.

Nick looked down at the ground.

"I want you to help us build Brambletown."

He grinned. "Okay."

"Okay." I grinned back. And that was that.

A thousand pounds of rocks—gone.

* * *

We carried four stacks of crates out to the cul-de-sac, making a couple of trips. Dad gave us a drop cloth and we decorated two of the crates in a crazy rainbow pattern. I sprayed Brambletown Paint and Decorating in purple letters next to the crates.

"Cool," Nick said. I wondered what Mrs. Fanelli would say when she saw him. He looked pretty much like a rainbow himself.

"Ready for a test run?" I asked.

We got our skates and followed Summer as she towed Zack and Contact around the new-and-improved Brambletown in the bike trailer. Remembering my unplanned skating visit to Summer's neighborhood, I practiced stopping—a lot.

"One more loop, Zack, and I have to go home," Summer warned. "It's going to get dark."

"Kitty's already night-night," Zack said from his passenger seat.

Summer took Zack and Contact for another spin around our town. Nick and I took off our skates and sat on the curb.

"I've been thinking about some other things we could add to Brambletown," Nick said. "Maybe even a ramp—it could be like a bridge or something."

"I like that," I told him.

Summer stopped her bike in front of us. "Last stop, Rostraver Station," she called out. "All human passengers must exit."

Zack climbed out. He leaned his curly head back in to give Contact a kiss. "Night-night, Kitty," he said.

"Come back tomorrow," Nick told Summer. "We're going to have a lot of work to do."

"Deal," Summer said. She pedaled away down the street.

"Want some pudding?" I asked Nick.

* * *

A little while later, Nick and I were talking over our plans at the kitchen table. Dad was unloading the dishwasher. Zack cooed to a toy truck wrapped in a towel. He'd named it Contact. All of a sudden we heard Mrs. Fanelli's frantic voice.

"Nick! Nick! Where are you?"

Nick jumped to his feet. His mother burst into our kitchen and ran straight to Dad. She grabbed Dad by the arms. "My Nick is not home!" she cried. "Where can he be? I have looked everywhere!"

"I'm here," Nick said.

Mrs. Fanelli whirled. She pulled Nick to her and hugged him. Then she pushed him back. A tear spilled onto her cheek. "Tuh!" she exclaimed, flinging the tear away with her hand. She turned and hurried out of the house.

"I guess I should have left her a note or something," Nick said. "Now you guys don't get any dinner."

"Your mom was too upset to think about that," Dad said. "We can manage on our own for once." He opened cabinets and scratched his head. He looked in the fridge. "Eggs?" he asked me.

"Eggs, tuh!" Mrs. Fanelli snorted, banging back into the kitchen. She set a pan of lasagna, an antipasto platter, and a layer cake on the table.

Dad held up his hands. "Really, you don't have to—" he began.

"Don't argue with me, Dan Rostraver," Mrs. Fanelli said. "Nick, time to go."

Nick followed his mother out the door and down the path.

"Good work," Dad said after they'd gone.

"You mean for finding Nick for Mrs. Fanelli and getting us dinner?" I asked innocently.

Dad smiled. "I mean for finding Nick," he said. "Your friend Nick."

I took a sweet cherry tomato from the antipasto and popped it into my mouth. The good news—and the bad news—was that Nick and I would have to go back to *pretending* not to be friends in school. I picked a hot pepper from the platter and turned it around by the stem. Now Summer and Nick were friends, too, and I wasn't so sure Summer was good at that kind of pretending.

I closed my eyes tight and took a bite of fire.

17

ALMOST A REGULAR
ANY-OLD DAY

Ready?" Nick called through the screen door the next
morning. He pressed his nose against the mesh, filling
the little wire squares with freckles.

"Uh-huh." I shoved my plate of telltale cake crumbs into
the dishwasher. Dad hadn't said anything, but I knew why
Mom had left that fat slab of Mrs. Fanelli's cake at my place.
Cake for breakfast was Mom's way of stretching a special day
into the next morning. Yesterday *had* been a great day, but
today I just wanted to walk with Nick to the corner of Broom
and Laurel, sit across from him at school with breathable air
moving between us, and have a regular, any-old day.

I slung my backpack over my shoulder and went outside.
Ragged gray clouds spun across the sky, and my hair swirled
up into the wind. Nick was standing at the end of our driveway looking at Brambletown.

"I don't think rain will hurt it," he said.

"Nope," I agreed. "It's staying."

We turned onto Bayberry. Nick tightrope-walked along the
curb, his arms out for balance.

"Did you and Jess finish the *Spark* editorial yesterday?" I
asked him.

"I think so," Nick said. He hopped off the curb and back on again.

"You don't know if you finished it or not?"

"Well," he said, rubbing his chin, "we couldn't work on it much during that big meeting at lunch, so Jess was going to finish it on her own and e-mail it—"

"You're kidding!" I blurted out, then immediately wished I hadn't. The last thing I wanted to do was bring up the *Mr. Alien* disaster.

Nick shook his head. "I'm not kidding. But she's e-mailing it to Mr. Allen instead of to the office." He flashed me an apologetic grin.

"There's a good idea," I said. Then I bumped him off the curb. He tried to bump me back, chasing me to the corner of Broom and Laurel. We stopped at the curb.

"Hey, thanks for the potato the other day," I said.

"Sure."

"See you at school."

"Right," Nick said. "See you."

And we parted ways for the last several blocks, like usual.

* * *

This week's issue of the *Springville Spark* was delivered to Room Twenty in the middle of math. Rain sheeted down the classroom windows. This *Spark* seemed a little rough around the edges. In my opinion, some of the artwork didn't quite go with the stories and poems. Jess's editorial, "What Bugs You?" started out with insects and ended up talking about people picking their teeth. But Owen's poem about maggots really made me laugh.

Maggots live in what they eat,
Manure piles and rotten meat.
They don't have heads or any legs,
And so can't think to wipe their feet.

We had another mega-editorial meeting at lunchtime. The room was full of a humming, busy kind of noise. I took a bite of my sandwich. When I glanced up, Mr. Allen was smiling at me. Sunlight shimmered through the last of the raindrops. This was turning out to be a wonderful, any-old day.

* * *

"Your assignment for this weekend," Mr. Allen explained at the end of the day, "is to find one characteristic your insect shares with human beings and write about it in the form of a fictional story, a poem, a newspaper article, or a first-person— make that 'first-bug'—journal entry."

"But I've got plans this weekend," Owen groaned. "There's a Rotten Roger cartoonathon all day Saturday and Sunday."

Mr. Allen's black eyebrows shot up like arrows. "Then please consider this assignment as brain protection, Owen. Don't forget, fellow learners—you'll take your insects home for observation and inspiration, and then return them to their natural habitats when you've finished. Let's all gather up our things and prepare for an extremely entomological weekend."

Nick went to get his hellgrammite. I already had my pill-bug.

"I don't think my dead tick will be much of an inspiration," Summer said. "But I can observe the new ones I find right in their natural habitat—Toby's skin!" Lacey shoved her chair under her desk and stomped to the coatroom.

"Speaking of Toby," Summer said, "I think he's feeling a little left out. Okay if he comes over today?"

"Of course." I lowered my voice, hoping Summer would take the hint and keep it down. "Zack'll go crazy for him." I pushed in my chair and started toward the coatroom.

"Hey, Nick," Summer called. "You never met my dog, Toby, did you?"

I froze. Nick turned slowly. Silence stretched across the room like a rubber band. I stopped breathing. *Oh, no, I* thought. *Summer, don't do it. Don't say Brambletown. Don't say Brambletown.*

"I'm going to bring Toby today when I come to do Brambletown," Summer announced, loud enough for Mrs. Novotny's class down the hall to hear.

I hid my face in my hands.

"Bram-ble-town," I heard Max say in a singsongy way. "What's *Bram*bletown?" There were a few giggles.

"Is it a new game?" someone asked.

"Yeah—a pretend game for little kiddies." Laughter erupted around the room.

My jaw clenched.

"I made up stuff like that, too," Alima said. "When I was *three.*"

I lowered my hands and shot her a fierce a look.

"Maybe Summer and Nick play house in Brambletown," Owen chimed in. "She's the mommy and he's the daddy."

"It's not house!" I hissed.

Owen pointed at me. "I bet Nadie is the baby!"

That did it. I blew up. "YOU DON'T KNOW ANYTHING ABOUT IT!" I yelled.

"Nadie?"

I thought that might have been Mr. Allen's voice, but I kept on yelling.

"For your information, Brambletown's a place we're making for skates and bikes—Nick, Summer, and me. And if being in the big-deal upper elementary school means you can't have that kind of fun or you can't be that kind of friends"—I whirled on all of them—"then too bad for *you!* I don't care what you think!" I shouted into the shocked silence, "Nick Fanelli has been my best friend forever!" I grabbed up my backpack. "I'm sick of these stupid rules about what fourth graders can and can't do and who can be friends and who can't! Some rules are for following"—I nodded at Summer—"and some aren't!" A sob choked its way up my throat, blocking off anything else I might have yelled. I burst out of the room, ran out of the building, and pounded down the block toward home.

18
BUILDING A BRIDGE

Hey...wait...will you?" Nick caught up with me a few blocks from school. By the sound of his voice, I could tell that he wasn't mad at me for blabbing about being friends. He was just winded from running.

I stopped. Nick held out my pillbug soda bottle habitat, then leaned over with his hands on his knees and huffed.

"Please tell me this is a long weekend," I groaned, "so I don't have to go back to school until, like, forever."

"Just a regular weekend," Nick said.

"I'm never going back," I said. I kicked an orangish pebble as hard as I could, sending it flying to the next driveway. "You'll have to take my assignment to Mr. Allen. It's going to be about how I curled up at home like a hiding pillbug and never came out again."

"What will your dad think when you don't go to school on Monday?" Nick asked, ever practical.

"He won't know. I'll walk partway with you," I said, "and then I'll go downtown and get a job." I followed my pebble down the sidewalk and gave it another kick.

Nick fell into step beside me. "I think you have to be at least fourteen to work."

I rolled my eyes. "Let's just go eat cake." I kept kicking the pebble the rest of the way home. When we reached my driveway, I sent it skittering into the grass near our mailbox.

"Hey ho, buddy-pals," Dad said, holding the kitchen door open for us. "It appears to be drying up outside. What's the afternoon plan—more Brambletown?"

Nick and I looked at each other.

"What'd I say?" Dad asked.

"It's a long story," I said. "But I'm pretty sure Summer's coming over, and yeah, we're going to work on Brambletown."

I got us milk—regular for me and chocolate soy for Nick. I slid into the seat across from Nick with my back to the kitchen door. We ate our cake, which made me feel better, and talked about things we wanted to add to our skate town. Dad went to pick up Zack. I wished Summer would hurry. I couldn't wait for my brother to see big old Toby.

"My cousin has a couple of old skateboard ramps, and I'm sure he'll let us borrow them," Nick said. "I found a wooden pallet in the garage that we could use to make a bridge. But it has those spaces between the slats, so it'll need some kind of covering if we really want to skate or bike over it."

"Like what?" I asked.

"I don't know," Nick said. "Maybe your dad has something?"

I shook my head. "I don't think photographic paper will do it."

There was a knock at the door.

"Come on in, Summer," I called. I heard the door open.

Nick looked past me and his eyes widened. "It's not Summer."

I turned. Gordon was standing there holding a cardboard

box. He brought it into the kitchen and set it down on a chair. "Hel-lo," he said. "I've-got-some old things from-my-dad's auto parts store for Brambletown." He only sounded a little like a robot.

Nick peered into the box. "Cool!" he said. "This is just what we need!" He pulled out a stack of rubber mats, like the kind you'd put on the floor of a car. "We're going to build a bridge," he told Gordon. "These will make the perfect surface."

"Affir-ma-tive!" Gordon said. "And I brought these old hubcaps, too. I thought you could use them as part of a building or a slalom course or something."

I thought about the other night when the un-robot Gordon had been here working on the *Spark*. "Can't you stay and work on it with us?" I asked him.

He smiled, then leaned down to rummage around in the cardboard box. "I can stay until dinnertime," he said. Now he didn't sound like a robot at all.

"Me, too." Summer opened the screen door, and Toby bounded in ahead of her. "I can stay 'til dinner, too."

"What took you so long?" I asked.

Summer and Gordon exchanged a pained look.

"What?" I demanded.

"Well," Summer said, pulling on Toby's ears, "you left school, and Mr. Allen let Nick go after you, but then he kept the rest of us a little longer."

"Great," I wailed. "Now I'm not only a lunatic, I'm a lunatic who gets everyone else in trouble!"

"We weren't in trouble," Gordon said. "Mr. Allen just asked everyone to sit down in their seats without talking and think."

"He said he was going to time us—two minutes," Summer

said. "But he was thinking, too, and he thought a little longer."

"A *lot* longer," Gordon added. "So we sat there a lot longer."

That settled it. I really never was going back to school again. I put my head in my hands. Toby came over and plastered my face with his slobbery tongue.

"No, doggie!" I heard Zack cry from outside the screen door. "Don't eat my sister!"

19

JUST WAITING
TO HAPPEN

Pretty early the next morning, which was Saturday, Zack was pushing one of his toy trucks in the middle of the driveway when he saw Summer pedaling up the street. He ran to our kitchen door and almost went right through the screen in his hurry to try and get inside. He still hadn't recovered from seeing Toby lick my face yesterday, even though the big black dog had wagged and fetched and tried to win him over all that afternoon.

"Toby stayed home today, Zack," Summer called out to him. "But your old pal Contact's here."

"I like Contact!" Zack nodded. He toddled down the driveway and jumped into the kiddie trailer with the fat orange cat.

Nick and Summer picked up where they'd left off on the wooden frame for the bridge. Gordon was designing a slalom course. I started painting crates.

"Nadie?"

I looked up. Lacey and Max were straddling bikes at the edge of the cul-de-sac.

"Um, can we try your—your Brambletown?" Lacey asked.

I looked from her to Max and back again. It all started to make sense. I had to laugh. "Sure," I told them. "Check it out. But wait," I folded my arms and tried to look stern. "What really happened with that red money pouch?"

Lacey hung her head. "Max put it in my desk for me," she admitted.

"I knew it," I said.

"I thought no one was looking," Max said. "She always forgets her lunch money. I bike to school, so sometimes after Lacey gets on the bus her mom comes over and gives the money to me. Anyway,"—he pointed to his and Lacey's saddlebags—"we dug around in my shed and found some stuff that might be good for the skate town."

Lacey nodded. "Little plastic fences from an old flower garden. Max's mom has lots of them."

"Those are great," I said. Lacey was rocking back and forth on her bike pedals. "Why not go for a ride first?" I waved them toward Brambletown. They raced each other around the painted roads for a few minutes. I smiled to myself and went back to painting crates.

Lacey turned out to be pretty handy with a can of spray paint, and she only said "eew" once, when she painted over a bunch of dried-out worms. Max designed a park in one corner, using the plastic garden fences. We worked until the sun dipped behind the trees ringing the cul-de-sac.

Zack poked his head out of the kiddie trailer. "Ride?" he asked.

"Last spin," Summer told him.

Nick and I watched her pedal slowly around Brambletown. "Was this really ever just some empty cul-de-sac?" I asked him.

"Nah," Nick said. "It was always Brambletown just waiting to happen."

"Bye-bye, kitty," Zack said. He climbed out of his seat and waved as Summer and the others went home.

"Hey, Zack," Nick said. "What does a kitty say?"

"*Huh, huh, huh.*" Zack made a very quiet panting sound.

"Poor Contact. She must be tired out from working on Brambletown," I said.

"Contact didn't work, Nadie," Zack said. "She sleeped."

"She has the right idea," Nick said with a yawn. "I'm beat."

"Rest up," I said. "I've got big plans for tomorrow."

* * *

By lunchtime on Sunday, Summer, Gordon, Max, and Lacey were back. We filled in Max's park with every bit of green paint we had left. Mom brought out a tray of almond butter and jam sandwiches and went back in to make lemonade. Dad dragged a couple of sawhorses across our street between our driveway and Nick's so no cars could come near our town, not even to turn around. He carried out the extra pairs of skates from the sports photo shoot. Everybody took turns skating over the new bridge.

Dad snapped about a million pictures. "I'm going to switch cameras," he said after a bit. "Be right back."

One of the boys from Mrs. Novotny's class skated up. He zoomed across Brambletown's streets without a word. Then a fifth grader rode over, stopping his bike at the edge of the lot.

"Want to help?" I asked.

"Right," he jeered. "Like I play dumb games with girls." I

watched him ride away. The boy from Mrs. Novotny's class skated off after him. I pulled in a long breath and blew it out again. *Too bad for them*, I reminded myself.

I'd just started sketching some more plans when a shadow fell across my paper.

"How about if I join Brambletown?"

I put my pencil behind my ear and squinted up at Owen. He had this stricken look on his face like it was killing him to ask. All of his most disgusting and irritating moments flashed through my mind. I wanted to say no. I knew it was possible that he would wreck everything. Then, for some reason, Owen's maggot poem popped into my head. A laugh sort of sneaked out of me and I coughed into my hand to cover it. What was it that Mr. Allen had said about everyone working on the *Spark*?

"If you can share ideas and work together," I told Owen, "you can stay."

"Yeah, yeah, sure," he said, like he could care less. "I'll tell you my ideas."

"You have to listen, too," I said.

"Nadie," Zack called from the kiddie trailer. "I want a ride!" His timing couldn't have been more perfect.

"You can start by listening to him." I pointed at my brother. "He needs someone to pull him with the bike."

"But—"

"If you want to help..." I let my words hang in the air and bent my head over my sketch again. I didn't look up until I heard the *screek skreek* of Summer's rickety bike. Owen zoomed around a curve and I heard Zack laugh inside the trailer. Owen laughed, too. *The world is a funny place*, I thought. I shook my head and went back to sketching the apartment house.

A few minutes later I heard Zack's voice again. "No!" he yelled. He was climbing out of the kiddie trailer as fast as his short legs could climb.

Oh no! Why hadn't I kept an eye on Owen? I dropped my paper and ran.

20

BRAMBLETOWN RULES

What did you do?" I shoved Owen aside and picked up my brother. "No!" Zack cried again. "No, kitty!" A tear ran down his cheek.

Summer and Nick hurried over.

"What is it, Zacky?" I said gently. "What happened?"

"Contact said—" Zack sobbed. "Contact said *yeeee-ow!*" He imitated the sound of an angry cat. We heard an answering *yeow* from inside the kiddie trailer.

"Why would Contact say that?" I turned to Summer.

"Yikes!" Summer said. "Let me see her." She leaned inside the kiddie carrier, her Louisiana beauty mark showing below the edge of her shirt. "Well," she said, "better back up, everybody. Looks like Contact's having her kittens."

I almost dropped Zack. "Having kittens?" I cried. "Here? She can't have them here!"

"Oh, I guess she can," Summer said. She hitched up her shorts. "The trailer's small and protected. She has her favorite fuzzy blanket inside. It's as good a place as any."

I grabbed Summer's arm. "What are we going to do?"

"Do? Not much. She can do this fine all by herself," Summer said. "Let's just give her some space."

"I'm getting my mom and dad," I said. I hurried to the house, still holding Zack. "Contact wasn't being mean to you," I told him on the way. "She was asking you for help because she trusts you. And you got her help. Good job!" I gave him a squeeze.

"I yelled." Zack nodded. He sniffled, then smiled a little. "Can I pat kitty?"

"I think you can later, after her babies are born," I told him. I hoped I was right about that.

"Dad!" I shouted at the kitchen door. "Mom! Come quick! Contact's having kittens in the bike trailer!"

Dad came running with a camera. Mom brought out some clean towels. She had her cell phone to her ear.

"I'm calling Summer's house," she told me. "I got the number from our caller ID."

The whole Brambletown crew was standing behind the bike trailer. Nick stared through the clear plastic window in back. Mom gave Summer a towel, and Summer draped it over the front of the carrier to give Contact more privacy. Everyone kept so quiet you could hear the big orange cat panting.

"Do all of your cats do this?" I whispered to Summer. "You must have kittens everywhere in your house!"

"Nah." Summer shook her head. "We've only had a couple of litters. We get our cats fixed so they don't have kittens. Contact was in rough shape when I found her. At first, she looked too old for kittens. But then we found out she was already pregnant."

Nick took Zack and motioned for me to step closer and look. Mom, Dad, and I peered through the plastic window. Contact's fur was damp and matted and her sides were heaving in and out at a frightening rate. I saw a scruffy ball of white and orange fur off to the side of the blanket. *Could it be a kitten?*

"Are you sure she's okay?" I asked Summer.

She smiled. "She's just fine."

Dad poked me. I saw a round, goopy bubble bulge out under Contact's tail. She licked and licked and pulled a clear skin sac away with her teeth. A wet mash of brown fur slowly took on the rough shape of a kitten. Contact licked it some more as it was born. I saw its tiny chest start to move in and out.

"It's breathing," I whispered. "It's amazing." My own heart was beating somewhere up in my throat. As I watched, a floppy brownish-red blob worked its way out of Contact. I lurched back away from the plastic window.

"From the look on your face, I guess you just saw the placenta," Summer said. "That helped feed the kitten when it was inside Contact, but soon the kitten will nurse from Mama Contact instead. The mother cat'll usually eat the placenta."

"Let me see," Owen said. He bent down and watched through the window. Max watched, too. I could tell exactly what was happening from the changing expressions on their faces.

"Whoa," Max said.

"Yeah," Summer said. "It is pretty cool."

Owen whirled on her. "That's—that's so gross," he sputtered. "It's maximum grossification! It's—it's grossazillion! *I* didn't win," he said. "*You* win." He took a step toward Summer.

I gasped. The gross-out contest could not be back on! I wanted to step between them and run away at the same time.

Owen scowled. He shoved his hand out and held it hanging in midair.

I watched a flush creep up Summer's neck and bloom on her cheeks. She pushed her hair behind her ears and shook hands with Owen.

"Now that's something you don't see every day," Lacey observed.

Owen wiped his handshake-hand on his jeans. Summer grinned.

I let my breath out all in a rush. My legs felt wobbly and I went to sit on the curb near our driveway. If this day held any more surprises I didn't think my stomach would be able to take it. Nick sat down next to me. Dad came over and stood in front of us with his camera. I hung my arm over Nick's shoulder, and he hung his arm over mine.

"Gotcha," Dad said, snapping a picture. "That's a keeper."

Lacey straightened and moved away from the back of the trailer. She looked like she was in some kind of trance. "I can't believe I just saw that," she said. "It's—it's—"

"Super disgusto?" Owen offered. "Revoltamatic?"

"It's beautiful," Lacey sighed.

I smiled.

"That's it," Summer called loudly from next to the kiddie trailer. "Five kittens, and every single one's okay."

She got on her bike and slowly towed her precious cargo into the shade at the edge of our driveway. Nick, Zack, and I followed. Gordon, Max, Lacey, and Owen headed back onto the streets of Brambletown. An old minivan pulled into our driveway, and Summer's sister got out of the passenger side.

"Leave it to old Contact to drop her kittens in a bike trailer," Summer's sister said, shaking her pink head.

Summer's mom got out of the driver's side of the van and hugged Summer. She held her long hair back with her hand and peeked under the towel on the bike trailer. Then she sent a familiar, wide-open smile all around. "Thanks for calling me," she said to my mom.

"I want to pat kitty," Zack said.

"Come on over here," Summer told him. She lifted the towel and my brother put his head and shoulders inside.

"Okay, kitty," Zack crooned. "Okay, kitty."

"What does the kitty say?" Nick asked.

There was no answer. I got worried. Would Contact be mad that Zack was getting so close? "Hey, Zack," I asked. "What does the kitty say?"

Zack pulled his head out of the carrier. "She says *prrrrr*," he announced happily. "And baby kitties say *meep, meep, meep*."

We all laughed. Summer's mom ruffled Zack's blond curls.

"Maybe we should add a column to the *Spark* called 'the Brambletown News,'" I said. "We could report on events, chart our progress, get new ideas and suggestions—stuff like that."

"The Brambletown News, huh?" Nick elbowed me in the ribs. "Does this mean you're actually going back to school?"

"I might," I said.

* * *

All along our way to school the next morning, Nick and I brainstormed ideas for the Brambletown News column.

"What do you think about putting in a map of all the skating roads and buildings and everything?" I asked.

"Yeah—you could do a great drawing of it," Nick said. "I could interview the kids who helped this weekend."

"That's a really good idea," I told him. "The Brambletown News is going to be the best section in the *Spark* yet!"

We stopped at the corner of Broom and Laurel. The morning sun caught shiny flecks all over the sidewalk.

"But…" Nick said, thinking out loud. "Say I interview Gordon, Max, Jess, Summer, and even Owen…and we put the column in the school paper. Then everyone will know we all made it *together*." He rubbed his head, then looked both ways to get ready to cross and walk the longer way, up Broom, like he always did.

I thought about all of the kids working and playing and watching those amazing kittens enter the world—our world—the day before.

"Exactly," I said. "Together. Brambletown rules."

Nick nodded slowly. "Right," he said. "Okay, then."

I hooked my arm through his, and he let me pull him a couple of steps along my way to school. Then I let go, bent my knees, and pointed down Laurel. "Ready?"

Nick grinned. "Set—"

"Go!" we shouted.

He didn't turn onto Broom. Instead we ran as fast as we could down Laurel and raced each other all the way to school.